"Kevin, is supposed to be," Emily murmured, "all the time?"

Before answering, Kevin studied Emily, who lay in his arms. Beautiful, passionate Emily. He'd never known a woman like her, so openly sensual and yet so innocent. So blunt, yet so shy. "What we have here is pretty unusual, I think. For one thing, I've never made love to a good friend before."

"Me, either. Maybe that's what makes the difference."

"Yeah," he agreed, not believing it at all. There was a magic with Emily. She was cuddled close to his body. He held her protectively, her firm buttocks curled against him.

"This is perfect, isn't it? Our own Garden of Eden." Kevin stroked her thigh, marveling at its softness.

Emily smiled. "Without the snake."

A familiar knot formed in his stomach. There was a snake, all right. Himself.

Bobby Hutchinson grew up in the Elk Valley, a breathtakingly beautiful region in British Columbia. Although her favorite subjects in high school were English and creative writing, she was hesitant about admitting her dream of being a writer. It remained a dream until 1984 when Bobby sold her first book, *Sheltering Bridges,* to Harlequin Superromance. And she's been going gangbusters since then! On a visit back home last summer, this talented author decided Elk Valley was the perfect setting for a romance—*Hot Developments*. Enjoy!

Books by Bobby Hutchinson

HOT DEVELOPMENTS

BOBBY HUTCHINSON

Harlequin Books

TORONTO • NEW YORK • LONDON
AMSTERDAM • PARIS • SYDNEY • HAMBURG
STOCKHOLM • ATHENS • TOKYO • MILAN
MADRID • WARSAW • BUDAPEST • AUCKLAND

Published January 1993

ISBN 0-373-25526-8

HOT DEVELOPMENTS

1

TEN FORTY-FIVE, and still no sign of anyone.

Kevin Richardson checked his watch again and swore under his breath. Where the hell was his ride? He hated wasting what he considered an invaluable asset—his precious time.

The small company plane that had brought him to this rugged southeastern corner of British Columbia had refueled and taken off for Vancouver more than an hour ago, leaving him at the mercy of people who obviously had no sense of responsibility.

The early May morning had turned suddenly overcast, and a brisk icy wind tunneled between the towering Rockies that rimmed the Elk Valley. Kevin shoved his arms into the sheepskin lined jacket he'd been carrying, zipping it and turning the collar up around his ears. Soon even the red-hot anger he felt at these Parker people wasn't going to be enough to keep him from freezing.

Damn, it was cold here compared to the Coast. The elevation was high—almost five thousand feet. He squinted up at the snow on the tops of the mountains, and couldn't help but feel awed by the spectacular scenery. The grass in the surrounding fields was green, though, and the poplars were already in leaf, but there was still more than a hint of frost in the air.

He looked around again, narrowing his eyes against the icy breeze, wondering if there was any other means of transportation he could take out of here. The rough airstrip was now deserted—three small planes huddled forlornly under an open-sided tin-roofed structure, and the two men who'd acted as ground crew for Kevin's flight had climbed into a pickup truck and disappeared down the gravel road right after his company plane had taken off.

"You'll be met at the landing strip, Mr. Richardson," Gertrude Parker had reassured him on the phone in her gravelly, tough-sounding voice. That had been the week before, when he'd made the arrangements for this trip. He'd even called again yesterday and told her precisely when he'd be landing. How could she have botched it up this way?

He believed in schedules and kept to them. He'd never keep anyone waiting like this.

He glanced at his watch again and shook his head in disgust.

Obviously, these Parkers who ran Elk Valley Adventures had never heard of schedules; making him wait tagged them as not only amateurs, but incompetent into the bargain. That fact sure as hell helped ease the pangs of guilt he'd felt over his company's plans to put them out of business.

He'd never had a strong stomach for the harsher aspects of development and it had bothered him that Elk

Valley Adventures was doomed—thanks to Pace Development Corporation. Three weeks ago, the corporation had snapped up the lease on the government land previously leased to Elk Valley Adventures.

"That's business, that's how it's done." Kevin could hear his father's gruff, impatient voice. "We're developers. It goes with the territory, for God's sake. Besides, the area's ripe."

Kevin had to admit that Barney was usually right. Pace Developments had risen from obscurity to its present position as one of the more promising young companies on the stock market because of Barney's killer instincts about land.

But Kevin was also aware that the company wouldn't have succeeded without his own engineering skills and ability to put together a prospectus that would dazzle hardened businessmen. Unlike his father, though, he didn't enjoy succeeding because someone else had failed.

He and Barney were poles apart in so many ways, even though Kevin had come to work for him with the express purpose of forming some sort of bond with his father.

Kevin shook his head, remembering. That dream had sure as hell died a slow death over the years. Still, they managed to work well together.

And working well together was *some*thing.

Not very damned much, but something.

"DAMNATION." Emily's hands were covered with grease and liberally coated with dirt from changing the rear tire of the Jeep four-wheel drive. She'd tried to rub the worst of it off on a rag, but it was useless. She glanced down at her worn jeans, fresh from the clothesline that morning, and swore under her breath. They were now filthy from kneeling in the muddy gravel at the side of the road while she struggled with the tire iron and the bolts and the spare, and she'd managed to get a sizable jagged streak of dirt across the front of her yellow sweatshirt.

She was a mess, but at least the spare tire was firmly in place. Well, maybe she'd used up today's entire quota of trouble, and the rest of the day would go smoothly.

Don't you wish, Parker.

"C'mon, Matilda, let's move it," she encouraged the Jeep as she scrambled back into the driver's seat. The ignition fired right away, which was a minor blessing, and the aging vehicle lurched and rattled when she stepped hard on the gas. She tore down the road, taking the curves at reckless speed, making the tires squeal as she wheeled onto the side road toward the airstrip.

She saw him through the dusty windshield. He was tall, wide shouldered, standing facing into the wind, thick brown hair blowing back from the strong, angular lines of his face. His two pieces of luggage were neatly stacked beside him. The man definitely traveled light.

Thank God for small blessings. Some clients brought so much stuff it took two trips to get it all home, never mind packed up into camp.

Emily waved cheerfully and pulled up beside him with a flourish, opening the Jeep door and jumping down in one fluid movement of her tall body. He didn't look any too friendly, but she ignored that and flashed him her finest smile.

"Hi there, Mr. Richardson. I'm Emily Parker. Sorry I'm late. Matilda here blew a tire. I won't offer to shake hands—I'm all grease." She grinned and held up her filthy, chapped hands for inspection, but there was no response at all. His deep-set dark eyes met hers without a trace of humor.

"I've been waiting for an hour and twenty minutes, Ms. Parker. Surely it can't take that long to change a tire?" His tone was as cool as the wind tearing at her braid.

Wow, was this guy ever a downer. Why did the good-looking ones always have to have rotten personalities or egos as big as all outdoors? There was some perverse law about clients.

"Well, I'm afraid it takes *me* that long—I guess I'm not the best mechanic in the world." She wasn't rude, but she wasn't going to take crap from him, either. "Let's get you loaded."

She reached for his duffel bag and suitcase, but he was quick, his movements lithe and easy as he gathered his things and tossed them into the back of the

Jeep. Then, to her amazement, he came around and held the door open for her to climb in.

Jupiter. A cranky, courtly gentleman, no less!

"Thanks, Mr. Richardson."

He gave a curt nod and shut the door. A second later, it popped open again.

"You've got to give it a real hard bang before it'll close—there's something wrong with the latch," she explained. Then she slammed the stupid door as hard as she could.

She was the one supposed to wait on him, didn't he understand that? A certain amount of the personal service was part of the deal. After all, he was the client; he was paying big money for the privilege of roughing it for two weeks in the bush. It made her feel as if she wasn't doing her job, having him act this way.

She couldn't help liking it a bit, though.

For some reason, she couldn't stop looking at him. His face had interesting angles and an expression of authority. His mouth was set in a firm line, strong and unsmiling, and his high cheekbones gave his features stark definition. There was a frown crease between his thick eyebrows, and his nose was slightly crooked, as if it had once been broken.

He was... She rejected *handsome* as too mellow. She stared at him as he came around Matilda's front and climbed in the other door, his movements spare and graceful as he settled himself and did up the seat belt. He moved well for such a big man, and he was big— six-four or -five, anyway. And built. Great shoulders.

She'd never realized before how close Matilda's passenger seat was to the driver.

"All set?"

He nodded. She swallowed and tried not to glance at his long, strong legs, encased in tight-fitting denim only a reach away. No sign of the familiar businessman's paunch on this guy. Below the jacket, his hips were narrow, his stomach as flat as her own. He wasn't wearing any brand-new drugstore-cowboy outfit, either. His Western boots were expensive but well-worn, matching the checkered shirt and faded Levi's jeans.

He turned his head and caught her staring. One corner of his mouth tilted up and he raised his eyebrows. She felt herself blush and jerked the key in the ignition.

Nothing happened. She mentally crossed her fingers as she tried again, and this time Matilda's engine roared to life.

Thank you, God. The last thing she needed at this moment was engine problems. She wanted to get this man home safely to Ma, and let her take over. Gertrude could handle him. There wasn't a man alive Gertrude couldn't handle.

"So, did you have a good flight from Vancouver, Mr. Richardson?" Her tone was cheerful, bright, upbeat.

"Fine." The one word was both succinct and final. After a long pause, he added, "The name's Kevin."

Well, whoopee. How intimate could you get? First names, no less. She gave it another try.

"Call me Emily. Ever been in this part of British Columbia before, Kevin?"

"Once, years ago." She waited, but he didn't elaborate. He didn't smile, either. He sat on Matilda's sprung seat, staring straight ahead as if imitating a sphinx.

"Don't suppose it's changed much. Nothing around here changes all that much."

No reply. She sighed. The morning wasn't improving any, that was certain.

Emily drove them back to the highway faster than she needed to, bouncing unnecessarily hard into and out of the deep potholes in the gravel road.

For the last twelve of her thirty years, her job had been making clients feel comfortable, encouraging them to talk about themselves, listening endlessly if they chose to dump their problems on her. She ought to be an expert at it by now. Yet as each moment passed she felt more and more uneasy with this silent stranger beside her—which was out of character for her. She liked people, and usually got on just fine with them.

But something about him got under her skin, making her awkwardly aware of his presence.

She decided not to initiate any more conversation— which wasn't like her, either.

Gertrude always said Emily had been born with the gift of gab.

But if he wanted to talk during the forty minutes it would take her to get them home, then damn his gorgeous, sullen hide, he'd have to make with the words. She'd had it for the time being with imitating Miss Mary Sunshine around this...this sexy, impossible grump of a man.

·

KEVIN FORCED HIMSELF not to turn and look directly at her, although he could see her quite well with his peripheral vision.

She had a streak of dirt across her tanned cheek that she must be totally unaware of, and the long-fingered hands on the steering wheel were nothing short of filthy. The nails on those hands were cut short, devoid of polish or manicure. She wore no makeup, her clothes were much the worse for wear, and she smelled vaguely of grease—not an odor that ever turned him on before.

So what was it, then, that appealed to him? Because from the moment he'd set eyes on her, something deep and basic and male had reacted like nuclear fission.

He decided it must be the energy she radiated that made him so conscious of her. She wasn't beautiful in any classical sense, although that luxurious, curly black hair escaping from the thick braid she'd forced it into— was it actually tied with a leather shoelace?—combined with her golden skin and huge green eyes was undoubtedly dramatic. And that voice, unexpectedly deep and husky sounding. She talked quickly, words pouring from her in a torrent, with a curious little hesitation sometimes at the very end of her sentences. She was quiet now, though.

He shifted on the lumpy seat and tensed his muscles to keep himself steady when she hit yet another pothole. He suspected she was doing it on purpose, and it amused him. He couldn't really blame her. He hadn't been exactly friendly.

She'd taken him by surprise. She'd bounded out of this deplorable vehicle like a slender amazon, all smiles and dirt and appealing curves and apologies, and he'd felt as if something had punched him in the gut.

Richardson, what the hell's wrong with you? Pull yourself together, here. The last thing you want to do is develop any sort of relationship with these Parkers, never mind having lewd thoughts about this one. This is business, remember? Serious business, big-money business. And it's probably going to get nasty before it's done—when they find out why you're really here.

She stopped for a moment at the intersection for the main road, carefully looked both ways down the deserted two-lane highway, and then pulled away with a lurch that threw him back in the seat.

He suppressed the urge to laugh at her antics, turning his head a little toward her instead, so he could see her more clearly.

She had beautiful ears, small and set close against her head. She wasn't wearing any rings—not in her ears or on her fingers. How old was she? He narrowed his eyes and considered.

At thirty eight, he was finding that more and more women looked impossibly young to him, and at first glance, this one was no exception. Her actions were those of a teenager. But up close he could see a few fine lines at the corners of her mouth, and there was an expression of maturity in her eyes. Twenty-six, twenty-seven?

Time passed and still she was quiet. Kevin began to rack his brain for something to say to her—something impersonal yet friendly, something that might make her think he wasn't the stuffed shirt he'd acted like back there.

But he came up empty, which wasn't too surprising. Making casual conversation had never been easy for him. What did he have to say, after all, to a woman with dirt on the knees of her jeans and old cowboy boots that badly needed new heels? So they drove for an extraordinarily long time in silence, the Jeep shuddering as it writhed its way down the twisting highway, up hills and through thick woods and out again.

Finally Emily couldn't stand it anymore and announced, "To your left over there is beautiful downtown Elkford, the new settlement that sprang up when the coal mines at the upper end of the valley opened up about ten years ago. Until then, there were only a few homesteaders living up here. My grandfather was one of them."

"Was he a miner?" Kevin had done his homework. He knew something about the history of the valley, how the rich coal deposits had lured settlers here about the turn of the century, how the small mining towns of Middletown, Natal and Michel had flourished and then disappeared in the mid-sixties.

Emily shook her head at his question. "Ma's father, my grandpa Luke, was a farmer and a hunter and fisherman. He started the business we have today—he was a guide and outfitter. My dad, Joseph Parker, was a miner. For a while. Quite a while, actually. He worked for six years in the underground mines, back in those mountains." She gestured behind them, to the south end of the valley where the early towns had been located. "He quit the mines because Ma thought they were too dangerous. He worked with Grandpa as a guide, but the business was seasonal and we needed more money, so he took a job as a faller in the bush. And he got killed by a deadfall, when I was twelve and my sister, Laura, was ten."

Kevin didn't know what to say to that, either. The irony of the story was both sad and touching. "It must have been hard for your mother," he managed, cursing himself for sounding stilted.

Emily nodded. "Yeah, I guess. But Ma's a survivor."

Kevin guessed that Emily was, too.

The small community of Elkford was behind them now, and the road suddenly narrowed. Emily didn't seem to feel the need to slow down, and once again, Kevin braced himself as the ruts in the gravel road became more frequent.

"Nearly home," she announced cheerfully as one particularly bad pothole almost made his head hit the roof of the Jeep. "Oops, sorry about that." But he caught the flash of wicked amusement in her expression when he made a grab for the dash.

Gravel flew in every direction, and Emily ignored it. Tall evergreens formed a verdant tunnel on either side of the Jeep, and suddenly parted to reveal a wide, fenced-off grassy meadow bisected by a narrow dirt road.

As the Jeep bounced and bucked on the dirt road, Kevin got a shaky look at a pole corral where several horses grazed; next, a weathered, dilapidated old barn and several other outbuildings whipped past. Then Emily braked abruptly in front of a sprawling two-story log house, set in a small clearing surrounded by evergreens.

It had a wide, covered veranda. Smoke rose in a column from the tumble-rock chimney. From around the corner, a large shaggy dog came charging at them, barking furiously as they climbed out.

"Caleb, calm yourself," Emily ordered, with little effect. "He's absolutely harmless, he just likes the sound of his own voice," she assured Kevin. She grinned and winked. "Ma says Caleb and I have a lot in common that way. C'mon in, we'll get your stuff later."

She bounded up the wooden steps two at a time, opening the door and hollering, "Hey, Ma, we're home. Ma?"

The house smelled of fresh-baked bread, but the woman who came around the corner into the hallway to greet them was anything but a plump, motherly type.

"This is my mother, Gertrude Parker. Ma, this is Kevin Richardson."

Gertrude's handshake was strong, as were her features. Kevin felt as if her piercing blue gaze might just be able to see right through him. Tall, slender, with wiry salt-and-pepper hair, she looked to be in her late forties or early fifties. But her body—clad in jeans and a T-shirt—could have complemented the face of a much younger woman. Kevin understood where Emily had inherited her striking figure. Gertrude greeted Kevin in the deep, tough, gravelly voice he remembered from the phone conversations they'd had.

"Matilda had a flat, so I was late getting to the airport. Kevin had to wait quite a while before I arrived," Emily commented, giving her mother a meaningful look. "I've gotta clean up. I'm a walking disaster area. 'Scuse me." She disappeared, taking two steps at a time, up a winding stairway that led off the hall.

Gertrude fixed him with a steely blue stare, and Kevin met it with one of his own. She looked away first, and he felt ridiculously triumphant.

"Well, Kevin, you made it here safe and sound anyway, so no harm done, right?" There was a challenge there, but she didn't wait for a response, turning instead and leading the way into a large, homey kitchen where a wood-and-coal range sent out billows of heat and a huge coffeepot simmered on a back burner.

"There's a washroom right off the end of the kitchen over there. When you're done you can sit down at the table and we'll have some lunch." Gertrude gestured to a large, round wooden table in the center of the room, already set up and overflowing with platters of cold meat and sliced vegetables, muffins, thick slices of the warm, fresh bread. The smell made his stomach grumble, and he remembered that he hadn't eaten since dawn. He headed into the small bathroom and was out again in minutes.

"You drink coffee, don't you?" When he nodded, Gertrude poured him a huge mugful from the tall enamel pot, waving a casual hand toward the cream and sugar already on the table.

"Make yourself at home. We don't stand on ceremony around here."

Kevin sat down on a wooden chair while Gertrude busied herself at the stove, shoving logs in the firebox and rescuing yet another batch of golden bread from the oven with relaxed efficiency that spoke of long habit.

"Where's Laura, Ma?" Emily bounced into the room, her face shining from a recent scrubbing. She had on fresh jeans and a plain white T-shirt. "Did Jackson turn up again to argue with her?"

Kevin was conscious once again of a shift in the energy of the room, and a shift in his own equilibrium, as if Emily's entrance had somehow made the world come more alive.

She took her place at the table, sitting on Kevin's right. The white T-shirt clung to her lavish breasts, and he studiously avoided looking at her, putting more sugar and cream than necessary in his coffee.

"Jackson's given up, and I can't say I blame him. Laura's down at the corral. She should have been back half an hour ago." There was annoyance in Gertrude's tone. "She went to check on that mare that's in foal. We won't bother waiting lunch on her—you know how that child loses track of time."

"She's a woman, Ma, not a child." There was something in Emily's voice that puzzled him. "And she needs to get off on her own now and then."

Gertrude shot her daughter a keen look but didn't say anything further.

"Here, Kevin, try some of Ma's bread. She makes the best of all of us. And this is Laura's home-canned chicken, and bread-and-butter pickles." Her hand brushed his when she passed the dishes; the contact was unsettling.

But the food was delicious, and he found he was ravenously hungry. Gertrude and Emily didn't demand conversation with the meal; like him, they ate with honest hunger, their remarks limited to everyday concerns about how much gas was in the Jeep, and where Emily had put the large cooler. But beneath the mundane phrases was a sense of deep affection between mother and daughter.

Kevin was having second helpings of everything when the back door opened and Emily's sister appeared.

He immediately got to his feet, nodding politely at the small, very blond woman who came hesitantly over to the table.

She wasn't at all like Emily. It wasn't only her close-cropped hair, which seemed to dance around her head like dandelion fluff. Laura was smaller, more fragile than either her sister or her mother. Her blue eyes were Gertrude's, but the triangular face, the small, neat features were entirely her own. Her shyness was evident in the way she moved, the way she held her head.

Her glance flicked from one person to the next, reading the atmosphere in the room. She wore jeans, with a bright blue maternity smock on top. Laura was visibly pregnant.

She was also deaf, Kevin realized with a profound sense of compassion as Emily's hands flew into rapid motion, making graphic signs to her sister—signs that elicited raised eyebrows, a crooked smile and a nod of agreement from Laura, plus a quick, assessing glance at Kevin.

"This is my sister, Laura." Emily's hands moved as she spoke, translating her words. "Laura, this is Kevin Richardson."

Kevin had seen and understood part of the "dialogue" exchange; certainly not all of it, but enough to fill in the blanks. He'd had a friend in high school whose brother was deaf, and together they'd learned the basic sign vocabulary, fascinated by the unusual visible method of communicating. Also, it had made a great secret language for the teenage boys. They could hold conversations right under the teachers' noses, or through windows.

He didn't feel comfortable about using his rusty signing with Laura, however. And judging by the exchange he'd just witnessed, it might be entertaining to freshen up his signing by observing for a while.

He cleared his throat awkwardly. "Tell her—tell her hello."

"Tell her yourself. Laura lip-reads." Emily's tone was acerbic, and to his horror, Kevin felt himself redden. He extended a hand toward Laura and tried for a smile that didn't quite come off.

"How do you do, Laura," he heard himself saying in an overly hearty voice.

"F-i-i-i, hank o-o-o-o." Her voice was high and uninflected and she released his hand immediately, turning away to fill a glass with milk. She took a seat across the table from Kevin and began putting food on her plate. She and Emily signed a few more sentences, and Kevin watched without seeming to.

"Wow, this one's a big hunk," Laura commented.

"Big pain in the ass," Emily responded. "Cranky like you wouldn't believe."

"You girls behave yourselves," Gertrude admonished, her fingers just as fast as her daughters.

But her warning did nothing to quell Emily and Laura's conversation. It was both pithy and to the point, and by the end of it, Kevin had all he could do to keep from laughing aloud. He'd also renewed his decision not to reveal his understanding of sign until later.

Much later, perhaps. It was sneaky, but he could learn a great deal about Emily and her sister as long as they believed him to be sign illiterate. And they were saying such fascinating things—mostly about him.

At last they paused, and suddenly an awkward silence stretched like thin elastic between the three hearing people.

Gertrude rescued them all. "Kevin, you mentioned on the phone that you're interested in photographing wildlife up the valley. I know you're not a hunter, but would you like to do some fishing while you're up there? The creeks are high right now, but there's good fly-fishing in the Elk River up near base camp."

"I'd enjoy that, but I haven't fished in years. I didn't bring any equipment."

"No problem. We keep a stock of rods and lures handy. Waders, as well. Emily'll see to it."

Emily nodded and gave him her cheerful smile.

"Sure will. And in case you're wondering, we'll be leaving for camp in about an hour. Most of the stuff's ready, it just needs loading in the truck. It's about a two-hour drive up to base camp. We use the truck to get up there and then rely on horses to travel to the other camps. You and I and Laura will be driving up. She's camp cook and I'm your guide. We have another party arriving in the next few days, so Ma will bring them up in the Jeep when they get here."

Kevin couldn't help feeling elated at the news that Emily would be his guide for the next two weeks.

He knew from the research he'd already done on Elk Valley Adventures that Gertrude ran the operation with a skeleton staff, rarely hiring more than two or three extra guides and a wrangler or two during a season.

He also figured that she and her daughters must have somehow gotten into serious financial difficulties. The license for their guiding territory had to be renewed each year, and this year Gertrude had allowed the li-

cense to lapse for over a month, giving Pace Developments the opportunity they'd been waiting for.

After meeting her, he was fairly certain it hadn't been
negligence on Gertrude's part. She seemed a compe-
tent, determined woman. It had to be money. One look
around this house spelled out that these people weren't
wealthy—not by a long shot.

It was quaint and wonderfully comfortable, but still
there were signals everywhere that money was scarce—
the antiquated cookstove, the wheezing old fridge, the
absence of a microwave, dishwasher, electric mixer. To
say nothing of the ramshackle vehicles parked outside.

Gertrude's next words cleared up the question of why
there was so little money.

"We'll need you to sign a waiver before you leave for
camp, Kevin, saying you won't sue us if there's an accident." She looked him straight in the eye. "You see,
last year one of our . . . clients . . . got drunk and fell out
of his bunk, breaking his leg in two places. The break
was a bad one, and he tried to take it out of our hides.
He sued us for plenty. Now our insurance company in-
sists on this waiver," Gertrude said with bald honesty,
handing the document to Kevin along with a pen. "We
take all the precautions we can, but there are still risks
involved, you understand. Read that carefully before
you sign."

Kevin signed, thinking over what Gertrude had told
him.

They'd had bad luck, is what it amounted to . . . and although they didn't know it yet, there was more on the way.

He knew that the women gathered around the rustic table had no idea that Pace Development Corporation was even now quietly in the process of taking over the rights to the thousand acres of parkland that constituted their guiding territory. That land, with government approval Barney had already tentatively arranged, would be turned into a luxury resort-hotel complex, with golf courses, swimming pools, nature trails—amenities that would draw well-heeled tourists from every corner of the globe. As Barney insisted, the area was ripe for it—rich, unspoiled, even romantic, with its history of coal mining and Indian tribes and early settlers.

Development such as Pace envisioned would benefit the entire area, creating jobs and opportunity for secondary industries, Kevin reminded himself.

The end justified the means.

He glanced up just then and caught Laura's wide blue gaze, focused on him. She smiled—a small, questioning smile—and the chocolate cake he'd been enjoying a moment before suddenly turned to glue in his throat.

2

TRUE TO HER WORD, Emily had them on the road in just over an hour, driving steadily through tunnels of evergreens that parted only now and then to allow glimpses of the Elk River.

There was wild game everywhere, and Kevin was surprised by the quantity and variety. Deer bounded across the road, a fat porcupine waddled huffily into the undergrowth, a herd of elk went pelting into the trees, and as Emily explained it, there were so many snowshoe rabbits along this stretch of road, she and Laura called it Jackrabbit Alley.

IF KEVIN HAD pigeonholed her earlier that morning as a wild and speedy driver, he must be doing a double take now, Emily thought smugly. She was driving exceptionally slow. What passed for the "road" was little more than an atrocious dirt path, and she maneuvered the battered green half-ton truck as though her cargo were as fragile as long-stemmed crystal.

In fact it was, in her opinion. Laura sat wedged firmly between her and Kevin on the narrow seat of the truck, seat belt curved across her rounded middle. Although Emily knew that jouncing over rough roads didn't induce labor, she wasn't about to take the slightest chance concerning her sister's condition.

Both Emily and Gertrude had done their best to convince Laura that she ought to stay home and close to her doctor—to no avail. When Laura made up her mind to something, there was no changing it.

Not that Laura was as fragile as she appeared. Emily knew that her sister was as healthy and robust as any young mother-to-be. The doctor had confirmed it, while not exactly recommending this trip, since the baby was due in six weeks.

Still, Emily was being careful, as was Gertrude. In the back of the truck was the one extravagance any of them had purchased in months: a sophisticated portable telephone unit that could connect their base camp with the emergency helicopter service that could bring medical help within an hour if necessary.

"The river's really high this year," Emily commented, freeing one hand from the wheel a moment to tell Laura what she'd said.

None of them had talked much since leaving the homestead, not since she and Laura had wickedly discussed Kevin in sign over lunch, right under his nose.

"Good-looking," Laura had declared, her face carefully impassive. "Macho man instead of wimp, like usual. Why pain in the ass? Make a pass at you, you should be so lucky?" she'd added.

"No way," Emily had responded emphatically. "Too uptight for that. Gorgeous buns, good teeth, great hair, deep sexy voice, wonderful thighs, but also big com-

plainer, when he talks at all. Needs a happy pill." Laura
had been unable to hide her laughter at that, and Gertrude had given them a warning.

Emily was aware now of Kevin's arm draped across
the back of the seat, missing Laura's shoulders but en-
countering hers now and then. His fingers had grazed
her neck several times, and the contact made shivers
run down her arm.

It irritated her. Why should this one particular man
affect her so drastically, and in such a physical way? She
wasn't a teenager, for cripes' sake. She'd had her share
of male friends, and one near-miss too many as far as
marriage went.

She'd even experienced her share of instant sexual
attraction, but the impulse had always fizzled and died
away soon after she really got to know the man.

She'd been seriously involved with two men during
the past ten years, and both of them, when the ending
was in sight, had expressed the opinion that she was too
strong.

Too strong for what? Why should she have to be
weak just to make them feel macho?

And what was it with her and men, anyway? For that
matter, what was it with *Laura* and men—or *Gertrude*
and men, if it came down to it? Their mother had had
more than her share of admirers over the years, but
she'd never remarried. Poor old Sam Lucas was the latest, and Emily would bet money that her mother would
send him packing back to San Diego and his veterinary practice before long.

And look at Laura—determined to be a single mother, deliberately choosing that route and stubbornly sticking with it, despite the obvious devotion of the baby's father, Jackson Briggs.

Emily had found herself feeling sorry for big, gentle Jackson more than once during the past few months. Her sister was impossible at times, hiding behind her deafness when it served the purpose.

Emily was beginning to believe that Gertrude had passed on some weird genes to both her daughters—something that kept the Parker women from forming lasting, stable relationships with the male of the species. Could genetic engineering do anything about a situation like—

"Watch it!" Kevin's sharp warning came an instant after Emily hit the brakes. Imperceptibly, she'd picked up speed for the past few miles. Now the truck had rounded a corner, and a massive elk suddenly appeared in front of them, directly in the center of the road.

They came to a stop mere inches from the animal, and it brazenly stared at the vehicle for a long, haughty moment before leaping into the woods.

"Damn!" Emily scowled, annoyed with herself.

Kevin had thrown a protective arm in front of Laura, making certain she wouldn't be thrust violently forward against the seat belt that spanned her round belly. Emily gave him a grateful look and Laura sent a shy smile his way and made the sign for "thank you."

"Sorry, you two," Emily apologized to her passengers, silently cursing herself for daydreaming instead of paying close attention to the road and her driving. "Those animals are a menace. There's so many of them this year. There's been a population explosion among the wild game the past couple of seasons." She put the truck in gear and drove off, even slower than before.

"I'd have thought hunting would have had the exact opposite effect," Kevin commented.

"Not at all. The hunting is strictly monitored by the game commission. I'm sure there's just as many wild animals now as there were when we were kids, right, Laura?"

Laura's fist moved up and down in assent.

"Did you come up here even then?" Kevin sounded curious.

"Sure. Dad used to bring us with him on fishing trips, and after he died and Ma took over the territory, we spent most of our summers up here."

"What a great way to grow up." His tone sounded almost wistful, and Emily glanced over at him. But he was staring straight ahead, with no visible emotion on his rugged features.

"Are you kidding? When we were teenagers, Laura and I used to wish we could have friends our own age instead of always being with Ma and the hunters, right, Laura?" Emily's right hand translated what was being said for her sister's benefit. "But we learned about the wilderness, we learned to cook and fish and clean game. Eventually to guide. We survived."

Conversation lagged as they navigated a minor washout on the road and started up a long, steep hill.

"You both chose to stay on here after you grew up, though." Kevin's words were more statement than question, which surprised Emily. She hadn't thought he was at all interested in her life. "Didn't you ever want to get away, to leave home, Emily?"

"Yep. Actually, I did leave. I went away to college for a year after I finished high school. Ma insisted. But it wasn't what I wanted, so I came back and started working for Ma. Laura did the same. She spent a year in Vancouver. She hated it. Neither of us adapted all that well to life in the city. We're country kids at heart, I guess. And for years now, we've been partners in Elk Valley Adventures—Ma and Laura and I—so our lives as well as our business are centered here."

Again, several minutes went by before his next question came.

"Is Laura's husband involved in Elk Valley Adventures, too?"

"Laura's not married. Neither am I. How about you, Kevin?"

"No." He didn't say anything more, and neither did Emily. She hadn't really needed to spell out her marital status, and worse, why had she asked him about his? There also wasn't any easy way to explain her sister's choice, and besides, it wasn't anyone's business but Laura's.

"So, what kind of job do you have, Kevin?" She turned the tables on him.

"I'm an engineer, but I'm involved in business—the investment business."

She presumed he meant the stock market. They'd had quite a few stockbrokers as clients over the past few years. She and Laura joked that such men only got charged up by their pocket calculators.

That thought didn't even cross her mind regarding Kevin Richardson, though. There was a rough, natural sexuality about him.

"Do you enjoy what you do?" He'd asked plenty of questions about their life. Emily wasn't letting him off the hook that easily.

"Yeah, I do. I travel a fair amount, and there's a certain degree of challenge involved."

She didn't say so, but she figured there could hardly be anything more boring than high finance. "It would be awful to have to do work you despised. I feel really lucky in that regard. I absolutely love what I do," she said. "I can't wait to get up each morning and get out into the bush."

Silence fell. The road wound up and down the foothills of the towering Rocky Mountains that encircled the valley. They crossed a log bridge that spanned the Elk River, and a long time later crossed another. It was a full hour and a half before they drew to a halt beside a sturdy log building.

"Base camp," Emily announced. "Finally." She felt as though she'd been driving forever.

The main structure had a wide, covered porch that held stacks of neatly piled firewood. There were also six small cabins scattered among the trees, an equipment shed, several outhouses, and a snug little building that housed a sauna. The buildings, all made of logs, were roofed with rough cedar shakes. They nestled in a grassy meadow beside the rushing river, and in every direction was a breathtaking vista of snowcapped peaks and tall pines.

"Hey, Laura, Phoebe's watching for you. She's Laura's mare," Emily explained to Kevin. "Phoebe's convinced Laura's her mother."

The small gray mare as well as the other horses in the pole corral came trotting over to the fence as Laura hurried toward them, crooning a wordless greeting.

Kevin slowly spun around, looking in every direction. "It's awesome," he breathed, and Emily smiled at him, ridiculously pleased that he recognized and appreciated the beauty of the valley.

Emily began unloading the supplies from the back of the truck and Kevin immediately joined her, lifting out boxes and sacks and cases of food, bedrolls and fishing equipment and several saddles.

"You don't have to do this, you know," she reminded him. "You're a guest here. You can go for a walk or just explore camp if you want. Laura and I are quite capable—"

"I'm sure you are. Now stop wasting your breath and let's get this stuff put away." He actually grinned at her—a beguiling, crooked grin that made her wonder how she'd ever thought him stern.

Laura joined them, and they worked companionably, carrying things into the cookhouse and storing them in the large, shelved room at the back of the kitchen area.

The cookshack consisted of a huge room with a peaked log ceiling, long wooden table above which loomed the largest moose head Kevin had ever seen, and various comfortable armchairs and sofas. At the end of the cabin opposite the entrance door was the kitchen, separated from the rest of the room by a free-standing counter. It was dominated by a sprawling iron wood-burning cookstove set against the back wall.

Behind the kitchen was the storage room, well equipped with rows of shelving and cupboards for storing dry supplies and canned goods. It was superbly stocked; there seemed to be enough food there to last the winter, with some left over, Kevin thought, as he carried in yet another case of tinned vegetables.

Out front, there were windows along one long wall with a view of the horses' corral and the river. Rooms were partitioned off on the other side. One room had a makeshift shower and a sink, but no toilet. Another was obviously the cook's bedroom; it had a bunk, pretty yellow curtains and a dresser, and Laura had tossed her duffel bag in there. As soon as all the supplies were put away, she headed eagerly for the kitchen.

She soon had a fire going in the massive iron cookstove and a voluminous apron tied around her middle. Engrossed in peeling potatoes and mixing biscuits, she totally ignored Kevin and Emily as she moved efficiently from stove to cupboard to counter.

"Laura's a tyrant in the kitchen. She doesn't want anyone interfering or trying to help. Would you like a guided tour of the rest of the place while she's making supper? You can choose which cabin you want to stay in, too."

Emily led the way out the door, conscious of him close beside her. He ran a hand down the rough wall of the cabin, his long fingers touching the logs almost caressingly.

"Who built all this? The workmanship is excellent."

"Grandpa Luke had some cabins up here, but they were falling down. After Dad was killed, Ma used to guide and cook for Gramps, and when he got too old, she took over and changed lots of things. She hired two carpenters who were woodsmen themselves to come up here and replace all the buildings, making loads of improvements over the old ones." Emily giggled. "Gramps was awfully set in his ways. He nearly had a hairy fit when he found out about the sauna and the showers Ma had installed. He figured 'roughing it' meant as little contact with water as possible."

"He's dead now?"

Emily nodded. "He only died two years ago—he was ninety-seven. And he was active right up to the end, bossing us all and giving orders right and left."

She led the way to the row of small, shake-roofed cabins snuggled among the pine trees and opened the first door.

The smell of pine filled their nostrils, and the cabin was cool and clean, but there were no luxuries here. There was a double set of iron bunks and a small, barrel-shaped wood heater with a chimney crooking its way out the ceiling. There was one screened window, with a stack of wood and an ax for splitting kindling outside on the tiny porch. A row of nails served as a closet, and washing facilities consisted of an enamel hand basin on an upended box, with a pail for water beside it.

"They're all pretty much the same. So, which one do you prefer?"

Kevin chose the most secluded, which had a view down the river from its doorway.

"There's mousetraps up at the cookshack. I'll bait them with peanut butter for you later tonight. You'll probably have some company till the pests find out it's not safe to live here with you."

Together, they returned with Kevin's duffel bag and camera case, and Emily brought a fresh sheet for the bunk, a pillow and several towels. Kevin had his own down sleeping bag.

"In the six cabins we can accommodate twenty-four hunters, but we seldom have that many all at the same time. Those buildings over there are the outhouses. The one on the left is for the men. The storage shed is over here." Emily led the way and opened the door, revealing rows of shelving, all stacked with saddles, tack, fishing gear, hip waders, horse blankets, saws, shovels and a large variety of other tools.

"Down this way is the sauna. It's a do-it-yourselfer." Emily opened the door to the compact little wooden building. Inside was a small, sturdy wood-stove, a waterproof lantern, a tin box lined with large white stones, several pails for water, and benches on two levels to sit on.

"After a day on horseback or hiking up those mountain draws and getting soaked in ice-cold creeks, it feels marvelous to stoke up the fire, get up a good head of steam, strip down and just relax in here."

Kevin could feel his body tighten and swell uncomfortably at the mental image Emily's words evoked. He could imagine all too clearly her naked golden-skinned body, damp and shining in the smoky lantern light as she stretched her long legs in the hot, steamy room. . . .

He forced himself to abandon the fantasy, brutally reminding himself again of why he was here, of the purpose behind this trip.

He had to get a grip on himself. He *had* to stop letting this woman affect him this way.

Most of all, he had to squelch the uneasy feeling that crept into his stomach each time he remembered his real reason for being here.

A great many people were relying on him; huge amounts of money were involved; the potential for gain was enormous. And the setting was far more breathtaking than he'd ever imagined it could be—even after viewing photo after photo of the area. You simply had to see it, smell the air, feel the overpowering grandeur of the mountains in order to fully appreciate the magnificence of the valley. No question about it: a major development such as the one Barney envisioned would succeed beyond their wildest dreams.

For the twentieth time that afternoon, he told himself it wasn't as if they were going to take advantage of Emily and her family; they'd be paid exceptionally well for whatever investments they'd made in this camp, and any others they'd established in the territory. Plus, he'd personally see to it they received a hefty goodwill bonus, as well. Hell, they'd come out financially ahead, with money enough to reestablish themselves in whatever business they chose. After all, they'd worked hard here and deserved to profit from their efforts.

When he'd first arrived today, he'd jumped to the conclusion that Elk Valley Adventures was a slipshod, poorly organized operation. In just a few short hours, he'd changed his mind.

It was well run. He was surprised and impressed by the efficiency and imagination that had gone into setting up a camp like this and maintaining it.

The trouble was, part of him wished his first impressions had been dead-on.

A much larger part of him—and certainly annoying parts of his anatomy—wished even harder that Emily weren't so appealing.

He half wished that he were what he was pretending to be—a Vancouver businessman here just to relax and enjoy nature for two weeks. He wasn't good at "devious." Not at all.

"Come down to the corral and meet the horses, and then it'll be time for supper." Emily's voice broke into his thoughts as she led the way through the deepening twilight, walking easily over the rough ground, her hips moving in a way that Kevin couldn't easily ignore.

He drew in a deep, frustrated breath and let it out slowly.

It was going to be a difficult two weeks—for all sorts of reasons he'd never anticipated when he left Vancouver that morning.

THE SONG OF A BIRD woke him the next morning. It was still early—a quarter to six by the watch he'd hung on a convenient nail beside the bunk. He'd opened the window as far as it would go the night before, and the sound of the river had lulled him to sleep. Now sunshine peeped through the window.

It was time for his run. He'd trained himself to wake every morning at this hour.

Still groggy, he worked his way out of the sleeping bag and swung his naked legs to the rough wooden floor.

Damn, it was cold. Shivering, he hurriedly pulled on his running shorts, and was reaching for a sweatshirt when a cheerful female voice called, "You decent? I've brought a bucket of hot water."

"Come in." He rubbed a hand over his tousled hair and stubbled chin as he opened the door for her, squinting in the sunshine that spilled in with her.

"Morning. Did you sleep well?" Emily must have just showered. Her face shone from a recent scrubbing and her hair was still damp, curling around her forehead, but tied back in a thick braid. She wore a blue V-necked sweater with a striped T-shirt underneath, and the same snug jeans she'd had on the day before.

She smelled of soap and apple-scented shampoo, and she averted her eyes quickly from his near-nakedness, setting the steaming bucket down beside the wash-stand and turning toward the door, all in one easy motion.

"I always go for a run before breakfast," he said. "Want to come along?"

She gave him an amused backward glance. "Thanks, but I don't jog. I've got a ton of chores to do. Stay on the road and keep an eye out for bears. There's lots of them around right now. If one takes after you, find a hill to run down. They don't do so well going down-hill—their back legs come up over their ears and they tumble. At least, that's what Gramps used to say. I've never tried it myself. Good luck, anyhow. Breakfast'll be ready when—that is, *if* you get back." She wiggled her fingers at him and grinned provocatively over her shoulder as she swung out the door, closing it with a bang.

Kevin stared after her for a moment and then began to laugh.

Bears, all right. He shoved his feet into his runners and was still smiling as he set out along the rough dirt road.

"IS HE UP? IS HE cranky in the morning? Does he wear pajamas?" Laura's questions flew the moment Emily was back in the cookhouse. The stove was sending out welcome waves of heat, and Laura was busy mixing pancake batter and preparing bacon. The rich smell of freshly brewed coffee and biscuits hot from the oven filled the air.

Emily explained about the jogging and made her sister laugh with the warnings about bears, but the whole time her fingers were busy talking, her mind wouldn't seem to budge from the mental picture of Kevin Richardson wearing jogging shorts and nothing else.

What was going on here? Was she actually drooling over a client, for heaven's sake?

She didn't joke about it with Laura as she ordinarily would have done—it wasn't any joking matter.

She'd actually had to stop herself from reaching out and running her fingers through the thick dark hair on that wide chest. How on earth had he gotten that brown this early in the year? Didn't it rain most of the time in Vancouver?

His shoulders were impressively broad, his arms more muscular than she'd suspected the day before. And those damn black shorts accentuated . . . well . . . everything, rather than hiding it.

Them. Whatever. He had narrow hips and firm buttocks. His legs were long and strong and well proportioned, and she'd even liked the shape of his feet—

Feet? She was lusting after a man's feet now, for God's sake? Get hold of yourself, woman. The bush is definitely getting to you.

IT WAS LESS THAN AN hour later when Kevin arrived for breakfast. He was clean-shaven, and his damp hair meant that he'd made good use of the bucket of water Emily had provided. He was, Emily told herself, at least decently covered now in jeans and a plaid shirt, his feet encased in the worn brown boots. She had to admit this attire wasn't half as exciting as the black shorts, however.

"Good run?" She busied herself getting him a glass of orange juice. Then she rescued the coffeepot from the stove and poured a mug.

"Great run. And not a bear to be seen. You wouldn't have been putting me on, would you, now?"

She shook her head, handing him the coffee and trying to keep from smiling. "Nope. You were just lucky. There's bears behind every bush up here. Sit down at the table—Laura's getting your breakfast."

"You've eaten?"

"Not yet. We waited for you, just in case you managed to get back alive."

He sat, and Emily judiciously took the other side of the bench. Laura put a good-size helping of porridge in their bowls and placed platters of pancakes, bacon and eggs and golden biscuits on the long table before she sat down.

"We always have porridge until the fresh cream we bring up goes sour," Emily explained, pouring a generous amount over the hot cereal and handing him the pitcher and the brown sugar.

"I haven't eaten porridge since boarding school." He took a mouthful, then added, "This doesn't bear any resemblance to what they called porridge, either. Theirs was slimy and usually cold. This is great."

"How come you went to boarding school?" Emily was hungry. She reached for a slice of thick, toasted homemade bread and lathered strawberry preserves on top.

"My mother was ill. Boarding school was practical."

"Did you grow up in Vancouver?" Emily was using a form of one-handed sign shorthand to clue Laura in to the conversation.

"Yeah, I did." Again, he volunteered nothing further.

"Old zipper mouth doesn't say much. Like pulling teeth to get any info," Emily signed to Laura. Kevin glanced up at them and raised a curious eyebrow.

Emily filled the air with words to distract him from what her fingers were saying. "I thought we'd go upriver today—there's a falls you might like to photograph. And we could take the fishing gear, in case you want to do a little casting?"

His eyes were definitely twinkling now. "Sounds great."

"I'll get Laura to pack us lunches, and we'll leave right after breakfast. You can ride, I hope?"

"Absolutely. Since I was a kid."

"That good, huh?"

His eyes narrowed and he shot her a challenging look. "I wouldn't say I could ride if I couldn't, would I?"

"Ride, yes, no?" Laura queried, her gestures lightning fast.

"He says he's a pro. Let's give him Spook and find out," Emily answered.

Laura smiled—the innocent wide smile that fooled people who didn't know her into believing she was meek and totally lacking in guile.

"He signed waiver. Won't sue us, for sure. Better take antiseptic," she signed as she left the table and began slicing bread for sandwiches.

"Antiseptic, hell." Emily was eating with one hand and carrying on the conversation with Laura with the other. "Full first-aid kit if he's the greenhorn I think he is."

"I'll watch when he gets on." Laura shoved brownies and apples into two sizable paper bags in between words. "Spook is crazy horse."

"We oughta sell tickets." Emily gave Kevin a beatific smile, finished off the last of her pancakes and got to her feet.

"Kevin, I'm just going to saddle the horses. You relax and have another cup of coffee."

"Last meal, poor guy," Laura signed to Emily as she refilled Kevin's cup and favored him with a smile of her own. "Too bad. He's so-o-o-o handsome, too."

"More sexy than handsome, I think. That mouth was made for kissing. Anyhow, serves him right for boasting."

"See you in a while, Kevin." Whistling cheerfully, Emily headed outside and over to the corral.

3

INSIDE THE CORRAL, Kevin stepped into the stirrups, making sure he had a tight grip on the reins. The dapple-gray horse shied to the left, and Kevin could see the whites of his eyes.

"Whoa, boy. Easy."

The women hadn't told him the horse's name, but he'd caught it in sign language—Spook. He'd learned plenty of other fascinating details, as well. This seemingly docile gelding apparently wasn't quite right in the head, if he'd read the lightning-fast signs properly. And by the deadpan expression on Emily's face, belied by the fiendish sparkle in her long-lashed green eyes, he was certain he'd understood all right.

He quickly threw his leg up and over, making certain his boots were seated in the stirrups before he allowed the animal the slightest bit of freedom.

Which was a smart move, because the instant his grip on the reins loosened, Spook went berserk.

The animal bucked and fishtailed and careered from one side to the other, doing everything in his power to unseat Kevin. But years of riding lessons and a summer spent on a working ranch came into their own, and he held his seat, not easily, but surely. And at last Spook began to give up. Slowly, the animal tired, until, with one or two final token convolutions, he subsided, flanks heaving, head hanging down in embarrassment and exhaustion.

Kevin took control, urging Spook none too gently over to the far side of the corral, where Emily had taken her own mount and tied him to the fence. She was perched on the top rail.

"The rodeo's over now, so shall we go?" Kevin relished the expression on Emily's face.

Her green eyes were huge and wary, waiting for him to accuse her of exactly what she'd done. Instead, he met her gaze with an innocent, level look. From the corner of his eye, he saw Laura vanish into the cook-shack from the veranda where she'd been watching the show.

"Yeah. Sure." Her face grew pink as he held her gaze, and she stammered, "Look, Kevin, I'm sorry. It was just a little joke. You said you could ride and we thought— Well, I just— I mean, the ground's soft, and I didn't figure you'd . . ." Her voice trailed off.

"Break anything when I got bucked off? And even if I did, I signed that damned waiver, right?" He swung out of the saddle and tied Spook to the fence.

Emily climbed down and stood facing him. Her face was now fiery red. "You've got every right to be mad. Like I said, I'm sorry. Hey, you're a good rider. If you like, I'll saddle another horse for you. That one's sort of . . . well, not very predictable."

"Not necessary. Old Spook and I understand each other now. We'll make out fine." He patted the animal on the neck. "Right, Spook? No first-aid kit needed at all." His tone was deceptively light.

This time her complexion blanched as she absorbed what he'd said. "How did you—how do you know—?"

He signed, "Old zipper mouth not say much, just observe."

Emily looked ready to faint. "Oh, my God. Oh, Lordie. You—you—speak . . . You understand . . . sign language?"

"Right again. I'm a little rusty, but it's all coming back to me, the more I watch you and Laura."

Her eyes widened, her mouth dropped open, and an expression of absolute horror came over her features as she mentally assessed all the things she and Laura had talked over in sign right in front of him. She closed her eyes and groaned as it all came back to her. Then she opened them again and took the offensive.

"That was plain old sneaky of you. I can't believe you'd stoop to such levels. Hardly anyone speaks sign. You might have told us up front." Her voice was angry.

"But you didn't ask, did you? In fact, you didn't give me a chance to say much of anything. Within the first few minutes, it would have been embarrassing to both of you if I confessed, so I figured I might as well play dumb." He was enjoying himself. "Besides, it's been an education, Emily," he drawled. "All those complimentary remarks about my physique, and the not-so-complimentary ones about my personality."

Her cheeks were scarlet, her eyes snapping sparks. Her full lips were drawn into a thin line, and he knew she felt like murdering him.

Kevin couldn't help laughing at her. She'd been so damned cocky and self-confident, so very much in her element here. It was mean of him, but she richly deserved this. Besides, anger became her. The rich, deep color flooding that golden skin, the tilt of her rounded chin, the provocative set of those full lips. . . .

"It's nice to know an attractive woman thinks I'm sexy," he purred. Impulsively, he reached out now and grasped her shoulders, drawing her toward him. She resisted, but he was quick. "And those comments about my lips."

"What do you think you're—?'

His mouth came down on hers before she could finish the sentence.

He'd planned it as a light, teasing kiss—a way of getting back at her for all her smart-mouthed comments.

The trouble was, it got away on him.

Her lips were incredibly soft and sweet beneath his own. Her skin smelled like the heady mountain air, and he could feel the seductive warmth of her body close to him, the fullness of her breasts against his chest.

A kind of madness came over him, and the kiss went clean out of control.

EMILY FELT PARALYZED. She'd pulled back when he first touched her, trying to escape, but he was incredibly strong, much stronger than she'd imagined him to be.

Effortlessly, he'd swept her into his embrace, and he was kissing her before she fully understood what was happening.

His mouth captured her own, his lips covering hers, hard and insistent. Her heart began to pound wildly. She knew she ought to tear herself away from him, turn her head aside, knee him in the groin.... She knew what to do and how to do it.

Her desire betrayed her. Some part of her had wanted this kiss, had fantasized about how it would feel to have his tongue demanding that she open for him this way.

She was trembling. Her lips parted, and his arms slid down from her shoulders, down her back, encircling her, drawing her deeper into his embrace with seductive insistence. Her own hands came up hesitantly, touching his arms, sliding around him, letting him draw her closer, thrilling to the feel of hard, smooth muscle beneath the checkered shirt.

His tongue touched hers, and she felt as if she were burning. An explosion of need leaped through her, making her want to push closer to him. The kiss deepened, and she made a soft sound in her throat. His breathing was harsh and labored, like her own.

It was the feel of his arousal, pressing hard against her thighs, that brought her to her senses finally.

What was she doing? What in God's name was she doing, standing here in broad daylight kissing a client as though she were some sex-starved bimbo?

She tore out of his arms, stumbling backward and almost falling when her boot hit a stone. She staggered, windmilling her arms in a desperate attempt to regain her balance, and he was instantly beside her, reaching out a hand to steady her.

He looked as shocked as she felt, but she wouldn't acknowledge it. She ripped her arm from his grasp, and for one awful instant she thought she was going to burst into tears. "What—just exactly what do you think you're doing?" Her voice was trembling, and she struggled for control. "Who do you think you are? What makes you think—? I'll thank you to . . . to keep your hands off me, Mr. Kevin Richardson!" She gulped, which spoiled the whole effect of her outrage.

"Your fee doesn't give you the right to . . . to lay a hand on me. And if you do again, you'll be sorry. I can take care of myself, y'know. I've had my share of big-city guys coming on to me." Damn, her eyes were filling with tears. Blindly, she swung around, stomping over to where her horse, Cody, waited patiently.

But Kevin was beside her in two long strides, placing his body between her and the horse.

"Emily, listen to me." His voice was low and urgent. "What happened just now surprised me as much as it did you. I only meant to tease you, to get back at you a little for all those smart remarks."

She swallowed hard. Her voice was choked. "Yeah. Well, you sure managed that."

The worst thing was, it wasn't just him she was angry at. It was herself most of all. She'd melted into his arms, returned his kisses. Her innate honesty forced her to admit it. "It was my fault as much as yours. I guess

I could have kicked and screamed a bit," she added reluctantly.

"I'm glad you didn't." Sensing that she was about to erupt all over again at that comment, he held up a staying hand. "Look, Emily, it was just a kiss, for God's sake. We're not teenagers. Can't we forget the whole thing and be friends? We're going to spend the next two weeks together, and having you glaring at me like this isn't exactly my idea of a great time."

He was being reasonable, damn his hide. And she'd lost sight entirely of the fact that he was the client. He was paying good money for this excursion—money that the Parkers needed desperately.

"You're absolutely right." It took superhuman effort to agree with him, but she managed it. "You caught me off guard, that's all. So, this . . . little incident . . . is history as far as I'm concerned." That was the biggest lie she'd told in a long time. It was a wonder her nose wasn't growing this very minute. "Now, if you really want to ride Spook, we'll get going. I'll just run over and collect our lunches from Laura and we'll be on our way."

Collecting lunches from Laura wasn't all that simple. Emily's sister had witnessed the entire fiasco, and she wasn't letting Emily go until she had gotten a detailed explanation.

Her face turned white when Emily told her that Kevin knew sign.

"No way! Really?" She smacked her forehead with her hand and rolled her eyes. "We say many things not nice."

Emily nodded ruefully. "You got that right."

"He's mad at us?"

"Not mad, exactly. Amused. But I'm mortally embarrassed."

Laura looked thoughtful. "So why he kisses you?"

Emily gave an elaborate shrug. "Male dominance. Chauvinism. Who knows? He said he was trying to teach me a lesson, can you believe that? Now, please, Laura, where are the lunches? We've gotta go."

But Laura wouldn't be hurried. "So, why you kiss him back, then?"

Emily was fast losing patience. "How the hell do I know? Who made you the kissing police? C'mon, Laura, please. Make with the lunches. We can discuss this later." She frowned, remembering. "Not where he can see us, though."

Laura handed over the substantial bundles of food and drink. "Looked to me like passionate kiss. Remember, when time comes, practice safe sex," she admonished with a wink.

"You're impossible," Emily told her. "And you're also a great one to give advice about sex." She patted her sister's burgeoning belly.

"I know from experience," Laura spelled out with such a sage look on her face that Emily had to laugh.

THE ATMOSPHERE BETWEEN them was strained as they set off, following the general direction of the river. For a few miles, neither said anything, but gradually the beauty of the morning and the raw splendor of their surroundings relaxed them both.

Kevin had retrieved his camera case before they left and he stopped several times to catch views of the river and the mountains, always with Emily in the shot.

"Scenery's boring unless there's some human interest," he said when she objected to being photographed so often.

"Do you ever sell your photos?"

There was room for both horses to walk along the path, and Kevin had drawn up until he was abreast of her and Cody. Spook was on his best behavior, responding to Kevin's slightest urging.

Her question was difficult to answer. His photos were used in the company's slick, shiny brochures, designed to stir interest in Pace Developments newest brainchild.

"I don't free-lance, no." He sidestepped her question, and a feeling of uneasiness came over him—the same feeling he'd been having since his meeting with the three Parker women the day before. For a few moments, the blue canopy of sky seemed a little dimmer, the sun not quite so warm and welcoming.

He'd also felt off balance ever since he'd kissed her. He couldn't look at her now and not remember how she'd felt in his embrace, how soft and warm and smooth her skin was against his cheek, how urgently his body responded to her.

"You ever try photography, Emily?"

She shook her head. "I don't own a camera. When I was younger, though, I begged for and got a set of watercolors for Christmas one year," she said. "I'd decided to capture all this—" She swung an arm wide, indicating the mountains, the river, the miles of trees. "I tried harder and harder, one whole summer, but it just never worked. I knew how I wanted it to look, but I couldn't get it right. My stuff was stiff and amateurish, and I got frustrated and bitchy because it wasn't what I'd envisioned. So I gave all the paints to Laura." She shook her head. "My sister. She didn't even try to paint landscapes. She just had a ball, covering the paper with mad mixtures of color and creating flowers that weren't like any flowers I'd ever seen. She had no preconceived ideas, so she just had fun. Laura's like that."

"Has she always been deaf?"

Emily nodded. "Born deaf. It was tough on my parents."

Spook and Cody were ambling along the trail, neck and neck. After a thoughtful moment, Kevin said, "Tough on you, too, I'd imagine."

She shot him a surprised glance. "Why do you say that?"

He shrugged. "I had a friend in school who had a deaf brother. Most of his parents' attention was always centered on Billy, and Jason felt left out a lot of the time."

"So, that's how you learned to sign. Well, it wasn't that way with Laura and me at all," Emily denied. "We were always close. I learned sign language along with her when I was little—I don't remember a time when we didn't understand one another perfectly."

"Did she go away to a school for the deaf? Billy went to Jericho Hills as a day student, but lots of the deaf kids there were boarding students."

"She went when she was sixteen, for a year, but when we were little, Ma wouldn't send her away. She said it was like punishing Laura for being deaf. I remember her and Dad used to fight over it a lot. He figured she ought to go to a special school, but Ma won out, and Laura went to regular school with me. It was hard for her, but there was one teacher who knew sign language, and she helped Laura cope."

"Did the other kids tease her?"

Emily tilted her chin up and shot him a look. "They wouldn't dare. I'd have beat the snot out of them if they had."

Kevin couldn't help laughing at her choice of words and her vehemence. "So, you were a tough little kid, huh, Emily?" She had a surface toughness even now, but it was only surface.

"I had to be. There was only Laura and me."

Something in the earnest response touched him. "You protected her."

"We looked out for each other—you know how it is. Didn't you have sisters? Or a brother, maybe?"

"Nope. I was an only child." The path narrowed, and he drew back on the reins, letting Emily take the lead, relieved that there would be no opportunity for more questions about his childhood.

He was right. There was little chance for conversation during the next part of the ride. They climbed a rock bluff and dipped down again into a draw, then scaled the steep mountainside until they came out on a plateau, high above the valley. The view was sensational, but Kevin was beginning to realize that almost everywhere in this area there were breathtaking views to enjoy.

"We'll stop here for lunch if you like." Emily had pulled Cody up in the shade of a tree beside a small stream. She dismounted and let the horse drink.

"Sounds good to me." Kevin was hot and hungry. It seemed as if breakfast had been a long time ago, and he could feel the muscles in his legs and arms beginning to stiffen as a result of Spook's earlier performance. He climbed off, allowing Spook to join Cody for a drink.

They let the horses graze after Emily unloaded their lunches from the saddlebags. She poured lemonade from a thermos, handing Kevin a cupful. He downed it in one long, thirsty draft, and she refilled it for him, unwrapped bundles and spread them on the flat surface of a handy rock.

He sat on the grass cross-legged, munching his way through the thick egg-salad sandwiches Laura had prepared.

"Muffins? Oatmeal cookies?"

Kevin took one of each. "This is great food. Homemade tastes a lot different than bought stuff."

"Surely some of the more enterprising women in Vancouver ply you with home-cooked meals?" As soon as the coy question was out, she could have kicked herself for asking. Here she was again, fishing for details of his life. Why the dickens should she care?

But the disconcerting truth was, she did care—a lot more than she wanted to admit.

He munched on a giant-size cookie and swallowed before he answered. "Once in a while they do. But it's usually duck *à l'orange*, or some other concoction. Nobody I've ever met makes homemade bread or cookies like these."

"Well, obviously you've been traveling in the wrong circles," she commented airily.

He stared at her for several moments, not smiling, making her uncomfortable. "Could be you're right," he finally said. "And how about you, Emily? What circles do you travel in? Is there a steady man in your life?"

She looked away from him, down the hillside to where the river looked small and very blue in the sunlight. "Nope. No one steady."

No one at all, for the past year or more; but she wasn't about to admit that.

"You ever been married?" He was tossing the questions off casually, and Emily made an effort to keep her responses light.

"Nope. It seems as if we Parker women aren't much for marrying. What about you?"

"Once, in my early twenties. It didn't work. It only lasted eight months."

This information surprised her. For some reason she'd assumed he'd always been a bachelor.

"How long ago was that?" It was a sneaky way of finding out how old he was.

"Fourteen years ago. I'm thirty-eight now, I was twenty-four then. How old are you, Emily?"

He didn't give anything without wanting something in return. Not that it bothered her to reveal her age; she'd always thought women silly who played coy about how old they were.

"I'm thirty. I'll be thirty-one in August."

He smiled at her—a nice, teasing smile. "Still a child."

She made a derogatory noise in her throat. "Some child. Wrinkles, cellulite, white hair, failing eyesight, shortness of breath." She squinted her eyes and made it sound as if her next breath were her last.

He laughed, as she'd hoped he might. He had a great laugh—deep and hearty—and his eyes crinkled up in an engaging fashion. The lines that formed around them added character to his face. She wondered why he didn't laugh more often.

"Funny, I didn't notice you falling apart like this."

"I disguise it pretty well. Ma says that after thirty, it's just maintenance all the way."

"She must do a wonderful job of it. Maintenance, I mean. Your mother's an attractive woman."

Emily smiled at him, as pleased with the compliment as if it had been directed at her. "Yeah, she is, isn't she? Not that she actually devotes any time to it. She's always too busy to even go and get her hair done. Laura and I have to practically load her into the Jeep and drive her to town when she starts to look like Medusa. She always says it doesn't matter how her hair looks because she's the outdoor type."

Seeing they had unexpectedly achieved a degree of intimacy, she dared to add, "What about your mother, Kevin? What's she like? Is she the outdoor type, too?"

A kind of stiffness came over his features, and it seemed to Emily that a door had suddenly closed between them.

"She's dead," he said abruptly. He got to his feet, signaling an end to the conversation. "I'm going to walk along this bluff for a ways and see if I can get some good photos of that wilderness down there."

She watched him walk away, feeling terrible about having reawakened painful memories. His mother's death must have been recent, for him to respond as he had. But how was she to have known?

She cleared away the remains of lunch, thinking about Kevin Richardson. He was a strange man—friendly and warm, one minute; aloof and cold the next.

There was nothing cold about his kisses, though.

A rush of warmth shot through her as she remembered those moments in his arms. And he was interesting in other ways. He even had a sense of humor under that grim exterior.

She found herself wishing that he weren't a client, here for two weeks and then gone again. There wouldn't be time for them to really get to know each other.

And even if there was time, she told herself scathingly, what could ever come of it? She was a backwoods woman, by choice. He was a big-city businessman. The chasm between them would yawn wider and wider, the more they got to know each other, and one fine day when she'd fallen for him, he'd tell her she was too strong for any man to feel comfortable around.

It was too bad, but it was a truth Emily had learned the hard way. The life she'd chosen for herself wasn't a life that men from the city wanted for more than a couple of weeks; and she wasn't the kind of woman they wanted on a long-term basis. But she sure didn't want the kind of life they led, either.

Life was choices, and you had to give up some things to get what you wanted. And most of the time, what you had to give up was tough. Like sex with someone you loved, on a regular basis. She figured she'd enjoy that. And laughter and love and babies, a strong shoulder when you needed one to lean on, somebody beside you in the night. Sharing with a man who understood you, who wanted who and what you really were.

Kevin was some distance away now, crouched on one knee, squinting through the lens of his camera, and she couldn't help but admire him. He was good to look at. Like the wild world around her. Wilderness. *So, look all you want, Parker. Just don't touch, or let him touch you, again.*

4

HE WAS AWARE THAT she was watching him. He struggled, half-ashamed, with the powerful emotions the mention of his mother had aroused in him, trying to subdue them, prolonging the ritual of focusing the camera in a deliberate effort to gain control before he spoke to her again.

He was a grown man. Why the hell should the shadow of a mother he'd never really known haunt him this way? Why today, when he could go months—years, almost—without thinking of her at all?

Paying little attention to the view, he wasted film, clicking off shot after shot, getting to his feet after a bit and casually moving even farther away from Emily, turning his back so that he wouldn't have to pretend to take photos. The emotions he was trying to suppress rippled through him—anger, nostalgia, and a longing he'd thought had died along with his childhood self, years before. He ventured a glance back at Emily when he was safely shielded by trees. She was perched on a log, chin propped in her cupped hands, staring dreamily out at the valley.

The way he felt had something to do with her—with the powerful bond between her and her sister and mother. There was a sense of family like an invisible rope tying them together. It presented such a powerful contrast with his own family relationships, that bond.

He'd never had a chance to really know his mother, and what he had with his father wasn't even a poor imitation of what he saw the Parkers shared. And it bothered him.

EMILY WATCHED HIM WALK into the trees, and she allowed him a decently long interval before she called to him. After all, toilet facilities were primitive out here. But finally, as the sun dropped farther past the median, she grew impatient.

"Kevin? Hey, Kevin, you about ready to go?" The afternoon was passing, and they still had a few miles to ride before they reached the river where he could fish. She also didn't know how knowledgeable he was about direction once he got deep into the woods. It wouldn't be the first time a city slicker had gotten himself lost just going out for a walk—although, after this morning's run-in between Kevin and Spook, she wasn't as quick to label him a city slicker, either. He was more than able to take care of himself in rough situations, it appeared.

"Coming." His call echoed, bouncing from among the mountain ridges, and soon he appeared, strolling toward her with his characteristic loose-limbed, easy grace, not saying anything. He walked directly over to the horses and swung into the saddle.

"I figured if you wanted to get any fishing in today, we'd better make tracks soon," Emily told him as she mounted Cody and led the way back to the almost-nonexistent path. "We've got about a half hour's ride down to the river."

He didn't reply, and they made the journey in silence, dropping to the bottom of a draw where the river had carved a path centuries before.

Sensitive to his mood, Emily unpacked the fishing gear in silence, setting him up at a likely spot and leaving him more or less alone. He thanked her politely, but didn't make any conversational openings. He'd obviously reverted to what she labeled his "somber mode" again. She wondered if his mother had ever warned him that his face would freeze like that unless he smiled soon, the way Gertrude had done when she or Laura had a fit of the sulks.

His first strike changed all that, however. She'd taken her own rod upriver a ways, losing herself in the rhythm and grace of casting into the rapidly flowing water and letting her line drift, then casting again.

She heard his excited yell and reeled in, hurrying back in time to watch him land a good-size trout.

"Man, he's a beauty, isn't he?" Kevin was as excited as any fisherman could be as he held the trout up for her to admire.

"If you could catch a couple more like that, Laura'd cook them for our dinner." Emily gave a mock sigh. "But of course, that's pure beginner's luck, so I guess *I'll* have to get the rest of our quota if we want to eat."

"Would you be challenging me to a contest, Ms. Emily?" His eyes danced with pleasure, and he was smiling again. "What about a little fishing derby here? We'll just see who can catch the most fish in the next hour."

"You're on. But that first one doesn't count. You caught it before we made the bet. That was just practice."

"Okay. But if I win in spite of your rules, I get to claim a bonus."

Emily grew wary. "Exactly what kind of bonus?"

Mischief danced in his eyes. "I haven't decided that yet. Are you so afraid of losing that you won't go for a blind bet?"

She tilted her chin up and gave him a superior look. "As long as I have the same rights, of course I accept. Good luck, Mr. Richardson. You're going to need it. I hate to boast, but I'm a champion fisherman. See you one hour from now."

He looked at his watch. "Three-twenty, that'll be."

"Whatever." With what she hoped was a confident grin, she strolled off, then when she was sure she was out of sight, she made a mad dash for a pool upstream where she knew the fishing was always good. There was none of her earlier nonchalance as she cast her line into the green water. "C'mon, babies, come to Mama," she crooned.

"YOU CHEATED SOMEHOW. You had to, to land three good-size trout in just one hour." Emily scowled at his impressive catch.

She had gotten two herself, and she'd been jubilant, absolutely certain she had him beaten. "Where's that first fish? I'll bet you—"

Kevin shook his head and pointed to the other fish, strung on a line a few yards away. "It's right over there. Are you accusing me of cheating? Madam, you insult my honor."

He couldn't stop grinning, and she couldn't resist smiling back at him.

"Besides, how the hell does a guy cheat at catching fish?" His jeans were soaked well above the waders he wore, and his hands and arms were filthy. His brown hair curled on his neck, and the dimples she'd noticed whenever he smiled creased his cheeks.

"Okay, I guess you win," she conceded none too gracefully. Inspiration struck. "Oh, yeah. I forgot to tell you that the winner always gets to clean the fish." She dug out the pocketknife she always carried and offered it to him. "It's an old tradition in the valley." Cleaning fish was about her least favorite activity.

This time he laughed outright, but he accepted the knife. "If you say it's tradition, I'll go along with it. Remember, though, I still have my bonus to collect." He looked straight into her eyes, and now there was a gleam of speculation in his scrutiny. His gaze wandered over her face, finally centering on her lips.

Emily felt heat flow up from the neck of her T-shirt and stain her cheeks.

God. What exactly did he have in mind?

She'd been an absolute fool to agree to something that hadn't been spelled out beforehand. She felt as if her entire body was blushing, growing hot and fevered beneath her shirt and jeans. The memory of that morning's kiss was suddenly vivid in her mind—the way his lips had felt on hers, the absolute assurance and expertise of his embrace.

Would she have to go through that a second time?

She broke the spell that seemed to hold them, turning away from him abruptly and walking over to where the horses were grazing. "You do know how to clean fish, right?" she called over her shoulder.

He laughed again—a low, delighted rumble. "I ought to call your bluff and tell you I haven't a clue. Then you'd have to do it yourself." He moved the fish to shallow water and crouched down on his haunches, grasping the first fish and gutting it with practiced expertise.

Emily watched and heaved a sigh of relief.

When the last fish—rinsed and clean, inside and out—lay on a fresh bed of leaves in the fishing basket, Kevin scrubbed his slimy hands and arms with a piece of soap Emily produced from her saddlebag. He was kneeling in the gravel, and she walked over to give him a small towel to dry on, but rather than taking it he grasped her hand instead and tugged her down on the riverbank beside him. She sat, bringing her knees up to her chin and curling her arms around them protectively.

Here it came. Her heart thudded and she told herself sternly that all she had to do was remind him that this was purely a business arrangement.

But he made no move toward her, choosing instead to sit a few yards away, arms resting on his knees.

"Now, for the bonus," he said softly, watching her reaction.

"Look, Kevin. I'm not sure exactly what you have in mind, but I think we'd better be really careful here...." she blurted out before her throat dried up and she had to swallow hard.

She wished he wouldn't just sit there, staring at her like that. It made her horribly nervous.

"What I mean is . . ."

He went on watching her with a polite, quizzical look on his face that made her want to reach out and punch him a good one.

But what in heaven's name *did* she mean? She was stammering away like an idiot, and she knew her face was flaming.

"I just don't think it's such a hot idea to . . . to . . . Well . . . for us . . . to be . . . to get . . . involved," she finally managed to choke out. "In any way," she added primly.

He still didn't react at all. His expression stayed the same, and he just went on looking at her as the heat inside her intensified.

She wondered if he was going to suddenly reach out and grab her.

She was so hot she ought to just get up and wade into the cold river. This was horrible. It was so embarrassing, and he wouldn't help her out at all.

"Is that what you thought I was going to suggest as a bonus?" He raised his eyebrows in pretended shock and shook his head. "Why, Emily, I'm surprised at you. I'd never dream of compromising a woman that way." His tone was earnest and confidential, and he leaned a bit toward her as if he didn't want the gutted fish to hear what he was saying. "I've never had to, you see."

She was getting angrier at him by the minute. For a man who often seemed unable to carry on the most elemental conversation, he was doing a masterful job of making a fool out of her.

"Then exactly what *did* you have in mind?" Her voice was trembling, and she struggled to control it, consoling herself with the thought that her rifle was close at hand. She could always just shoot him if this got any worse.

"Well." He leaned back on his elbows, seemingly impervious to the rough gravel that was making her own bottom sore.

"Well, actually..." He drawled out the words and went on giving her that phony innocent look. "I figured that I'd ask you to teach me the finer points of signing. You see, it's been a long time since I used it, and although I can 'read' it fairly well, I think I'm pretty rusty at 'speaking' it."

She was speechless. She gaped at him, and pure rage rose in her. He'd deliberately led her to believe—

He'd made her think he wanted—

And then he—

"So what do you say, Emily? I did win the derby, re-member."

Only extreme self-control stopped her from giving him the one-fingered sign that absolutely everyone un-derstood. She looked away from him, blindly gazing out at the river for several moments, taking deep breaths and telling herself to relax.

"I know you and Laura use a kind of shorthand when you 'talk.' I'd like to learn it." For the first time, all hint of teasing disappeared from his voice. "I'd very much like to get to know you and your sister better, and that's not possible unless my signing improves a whole lot." He reached out and touched her shoulder gently with his fingers. "I'm sorry I teased you just now. It was too good an opportunity to miss, though, after this morn-ing. Forgive me?"

She tried to stay mad, but her sense of humor won out. She still didn't think it was fair of him; but then, her conscience reminded, neither was what she and Laura had done entirely fair.

"I shouldn't have jumped to conclusions." The ad-mission felt like she was yanking out her own teeth, but she made it anyway.

"So I'm forgiven?" His fingers were still on her shoulder, and he tightened his grip a little, enough to punctuate what he was saying.

"I'll teach you to sign." She deliberately avoided ab-solution. He'd just have to take his chances, because when the ideal opportunity came to pay him back, she was going to pounce on it.

The sun was heading for the horizon.

"It's time we started back."

He got to his feet in one smooth movement, reaching out a hand to help her up. She hesitated, but finally accepted.

They gathered up the fish and the gear and together began the process of reloading the horses.

When they were once again in the saddle, he said, "Emily?"

She was starting down the trail already. "What is it?"

"I wanted you to know that this is the most fun I've had in a very long time." His voice was stilted, as if he'd had to plot out the words and repeat them in a certain order. "Thank you."

Surprised, and more pleased than she cared to admit, she turned in the saddle and smiled back at him.

"Just doing my job, sir. Our aim at Elk Valley Adventures is to amuse and delight you so that you'll come again."

There was no answer, and she rode along for a while without turning around to look back at him.

When she did, he had his head down and seemed lost in thought.

"YOU'RE AN OPTIMIST, kid. What makes you think we caught anything?" They arrived back at sunset to find that Laura had a huge black frying pan heating on the cookstove and a pile of neatly sliced potatoes ready to be French fried. Emily teased her for a few moments, insisting they'd been unlucky.

"Hand over the fish," Laura signed, snapping her fingers impatiently. "You want supper, right? And I can smell fish."

"What . . . if . . . we . . . did . . . not . . . catch? What . . . would . . . we . . . eat?" Kevin's signs were laborious, but Laura was delighted at his attempts.

"Bologna sandwiches," she spelled out succinctly, and then set about finishing the meal while Kevin and Emily took turns in the washroom, scrubbing the grime off themselves.

Kevin couldn't remember laughing as much as he did during the supper that followed. He tried out his rusty signs, and some of his attempts reduced the women to helpless giggles. Laura was amused by the story of the fishing derby, although Emily didn't include the trick Kevin had played on her.

"Good for Emily to lose once in a while," Laura said to Kevin. "She always wins—wins at games, wins at sports at school."

"What sports did you play?" Kevin asked.

"Softball, basketball, track and field," Emily answered. "How about you?"

"Rugby, football, swimming. How about you, Laura?"

She winked at him with a decidedly lewd expression and pointed to her rounded stomach. "Indoor sports," she signed with a wicked sparkle in her innocent-looking blue eyes.

"She was so shy in school it was awful, and yet she makes Ma absolutely crazy when she says things like that," Emily chided. "Which is exactly why you do it. Right, Laura?"

Laura nodded. "Keeps her from getting bored," she told them with an impish grin.

Kevin found himself wondering how his father would react to these Parker women. Barney could sure use some of their lightness. There'd never been any teasing or much joking around between father and son, that was certain. Business discussions, yes. Freewheeling conversations like this, definitely not.

As the meal progressed, the two sisters grew almost giddy, telling tales on themselves about wild escapades they'd pulled over the years, making Kevin laugh as they mimed scenes to enlarge on the signed stories they related, interpreting for him any lightning-fast signs that he didn't understand. They were totally relaxed and uninhibited, and he found himself talking much more than he ever usually did.

Signing was somehow easier than speaking in words, because it was so direct. The effort of translating into the visual stopped him from mentally double-checking everything he was about to say; conversation tonight became less of a chore to him and more of a pleasure.

Outside, darkness fell, and the women lit several lanterns instead of starting the power plant. The soft light didn't reach the far corners of the large room, and shadows drifted across the log walls. The golden glow seemed to cast a romantic spell over the long table, and

Kevin found his gaze drawn hypnotically to Emily's features, intrigued by the way her green eyes, huge and luminous, reflected the lamplights. Her high-cheekboned face, devoid of makeup, to him was starkly beautiful.

"For dessert, chocolate cake," Laura announced. She poured mugs of coffee, and sliced huge chunks of moist double-layered cake covered with fluffy white icing onto their plates.

"You know the old saying, 'The way to a man's heart is through his stomach'?" Kevin asked. When Laura nodded, he groaned and clutched his middle. "Well, my stomach's about to burst, so God knows what my heart is doing."

"What about women?" Laura queried a few minutes later. "Way to a *woman's* heart is . . . what?" She held both hands out questioningly.

Kevin gave an exaggerated shrug, indicating he was way out of his league here. "No man knows that," he said.

Emily thought for several moments, savoring a mouthful of her cake, sipping coffee before she answered. "That's easy," she signed. "The way to a woman's heart is through her mind and soul."

Laura agreed. "Right. All women want perfect romance. Love, understanding, companionship, intelligence. But love for man and for woman can have different meanings, right?"

"Yeah." Emily nodded agreement, avoiding Kevin's eyes, obviously uncomfortable with the way the conversation was going, but determined to speak her mind. "Men are inclined to confuse sex with love, I think."

"But women want physical love, too," Laura insisted. "I think they're part of the same emotion."

"It isn't sex that's the big problem between men and women, anyway," Emily burst out. "It's wanting to change the other person, deciding that they'll use the relationship to make the other guy into whatever they figure is perfect. It's so crazy, because you can't ever change anybody else. And even if you could, you wouldn't have the person you fell in love with in the first place. It's insanity."

"You've got that right." Kevin's tone hinted that he'd had personal experience with exactly what Emily was describing, but before either woman could quiz him on it, he changed the subject abruptly. "Let's get these dishes done, ladies."

Emily got up and started to clear the table. "You cooked, Laura, so I'll the do dishes."

"Great idea." Laura wasn't about to object. She stretched and yawned. "I'll read in bed. Good night, you two." She took a lantern and headed for her room.

"If you wash, I'll dry," Kevin volunteered.

"Fine with me." If he expected her to refuse his offer, he was out of luck. "We won't even charge you extra for the privilege," she teased, tipping hot water out of the big kettle into a plastic basin and adding a squirt of soap.

They worked in a companionable silence in the dimly lit room. When all the dishes were clean, Emily put them away and turned the wick down on the lantern until the flame was extinguished and the room was in blackness. Calling out good-night to Laura, she flicked on a strong flashlight and led the way out the door.

Outside, the moon was full and the whole world seemed bathed in silver light. It was bright enough for her to switch off the flashlight; they could see quite well without it.

He was walking close beside her, and he reached out and took her hand in his. His strong fingers closed over hers, and the pleasure she felt was quite out of proportion to the simple gesture.

"I've had a fine day, Emily. I thank you for it." His voice was soft, gentle almost. He gave her fingers a squeeze that emphasized his words.

"It didn't start off all that well." She remembered the scene with Spook and couldn't help smiling in the darkness. "Where did you learn to ride like that?"

"My father sent me off for a couple of summers to a working ranch he had shares in up in the Caribou. I had plenty of practice at bronco busting, but that was a long time ago. Old Spook gave me a few bad moments there, this morning."

She was quiet, then remarked, "I guess your family was pretty well-off, huh? Private schools, shares in a ranch, and all that." She realized after the words were out that she was probably back on dicey ground, talking about his family again.

"We weren't rich, but money wasn't a problem."

"Lucky you. It seems to have always been a big problem in our family."

"Money isn't everything." There was a definite note of vehemence—and was there also bitterness?—in his voice.

"Funny how it's always the wealthy people who say that." Her tone was challenging—and annoyed, as well.

They were nearly at his cabin and he stopped abruptly, put his hands on her shoulders and spun her toward him. "Listen, I'd have given a lot to have had a sister like Laura. Or—" He bit off whatever he'd been about to say and looked down at her, studying her face in the moonlight. His hands loosened their hold on her shoulders and wandered up to stroke her hair.

"You're a beautiful woman, Emily."

In another moment, he'd kiss her. She stood quite still for an instant, wanting that kiss, and then she remembered his teasing earlier that day. Was he teasing her again?

She wasn't about to make a fool of herself twice, standing here and tipping her face up for a kiss and then having him laugh at her instead.

She twisted sharply away from him, flicking on the flashlight and illuminating the path that led to her own cabin. She didn't need the light; she could have found her way blindfolded, but the light made a barrier between them.

"Good night, Richardson," she called over her shoulder. "See you in the morning."

He didn't reply until she was almost at her own door.

"Good night, Emily. Sleep well."

She wondered if he was being sarcastic, because despite her tiredness from the busy day, the moon had set before she finally got to sleep.

THE NEXT THREE DAYS were filled with activity. Kevin and Emily spent most of the long, sunny days alone together; Laura would provide a monstrous early breakfast and a packed lunch, and the two of them would ride off, spending the day exploring lakes and rivers for the best fishing, or simply riding along the numerous trails Emily was familiar with in search of scenes for him to photograph. After that first day, Kevin traded unpredictable Spook for a spirited stallion called Lucifer, and the expeditions became pure pleasure.

"Exactly what sort of wild life pictures do you want?" Emily asked the second morning as they climbed a rough and rocky trail in order to reach a waterfall she wanted him to see. "I can't guarantee that I can show you every species of wildlife in the valley, but I do know where to look for bears, for instance, or sheep or goats."

"Whatever we come across is fine. I don't have any exact requirements." He felt the now-familiar jab of conscience at his pretense of being a photographer. He'd managed to forget the real purpose of this trip for most of yesterday. He was simply going to have to put it out of his mind for the next few days, as well, because there wasn't any way he could tell Emily or Laura exactly who and what he was. Not yet.

At breakfast this morning, there had been an easy camaraderie among the three of them—the result of their lighthearted conversation of the night before.

Emily now made sure he understood all the rapid signs she exchanged with Laura, although they both teased him unmercifully and corrected his own signing when necessary. He definitely felt less like a visitor and more like a friend—Laura's friend, at least. With Emily, there was that disconcerting awareness, that ever-present sense of her as a woman he'd kissed thoroughly—and planned to kiss again.

He was riding behind her on a narrow trail with thick forest on either side. Sunlight and shade dappled her as they moved through the trees. She wore a battered brown felt hat this morning, and her shining black braid hung below it past her shoulder blades. She had on a red, checkered cotton shirt, tucked into her usual faded, snug-fitting jeans.

He studied her narrow waist, the intriguing curve of her rounded bottom outlined provocatively by the thin denim, and the long, slender lines of her legs. She was whistling, parodying the birds around them with a soft, sweet trill, and it sounded to him as if one bird at least was answering her, call for call.

She was beautiful. She was also a creature ideally suited to her environment, he realized. She was unlike any woman he'd ever met—devoid of intricate makeup, smart clothing, any of the trappings and complex games he'd come to believe were part and parcel of being female. He couldn't see her face, but he knew it shone from being scrubbed with soap and water. She ran a tube of lip gloss across her mouth now and then, but he hadn't seen her use any other cosmetics. She smelled of apple shampoo and a fresh lemon scent that wasn't any perfume he was familiar with; other than that, her odor was clean woman, pure and simple.

She'd taken a set of field glasses from the leather case that hung from her saddle and was scanning the side of the mountain.

"There's a hawk's nest high up on that bluff," she called back to him now, turning in the saddle to point to a rock face on the left, high above them. "Maybe you can get a shot of the mother with your telephoto lens if we stop in that clearing up ahead."

She was excited at the prospect, with animation in every line of her body as she spurred Cody into a trot. Part of her charm was this enthusiasm, Kevin mused.

He followed and dismounted beside her, accepting the glasses for a moment so he, too, could locate the nest.

Emily's face was animated as he took his camera out of its case and focused, waiting for the moment when the mother hawk would swoop down to feed her young. As Emily stood close beside him, holding the glasses tightly to her eyes, he reveled in her simple, uncomplicated delight in the experience.

"There she is, Kevin! There she is now, just to the right of the nest. She's huge! Oh, wow, did you get that? She had a mouse in her talons, she gave it to one of the babies...."

The deep, husky voice with its trace of hesitation at the end of every rapid sentence was an Emily trademark. While he clicked one shot after another, she punctuated the pictures with a steady stream of commentary.

He'd always been drawn to women who talked a lot. It made it easy for him to be quiet. He'd been sexually attracted to some of them...well, more than some. But he couldn't remember simply *liking* any of them as companions.

He liked Emily. How could he not like her?

He lowered the camera at last and returned the exultant smile she gave him. Her eyes were as green as the pine trees they'd been riding through all morning, and her soft lips were full and inviting.

A sudden, overwhelming desire to take her in his arms right then and there and make love to her swept over him, and it was all he could do to take a step away and put the camera carefully back into its case, realizing as he did so that his hands were trembling.

He liked Emily, all right. Far too much for his—or her—own good.

"Great shots, huh, Kev? You'll have to tell me what magazine you sell these to. It'll be such a thrill, seeing them in print. You want a coffee now, or should we ride for a while and then stop for lunch?"

He struggled for control. "Let's ride. I want to see this waterfall you've been babbling about."

"I don't babble—I describe vividly. You're gonna be impressed. You'll see."

He looked into her beautiful face and wanted to tell her he already was.

5

THE THREE OF THEM had been alone for four idyllic days when Gertrude arrived with the other clients.

It was dusk, and Kevin and Emily were chopping wood for the cookstove and arguing loudly over who was more adept at splitting logs, when they heard the truck approaching.

"It's Ma." Emily let her ax drop to the ground, narrowly missing Kevin's foot. She raced over to the door of the cookshack to tell Laura.

When the truck rumbled into the clearing, Emily and Laura were waiting in the yard to greet the new arrivals. Kevin stayed in the background, amazed at the degree of resentment he felt over the arrival of the others. He wanted the camaraderie that had formed between him and Emily and Laura to continue just as it was.

"Hey, Ma, great to see you." Emily enveloped her mother in a bear hug. Gertrude wore jeans and a T-shirt, just like her daughters, and again Kevin noticed how very attractive she was. Her wiry hair stood out in every direction, and there wasn't a trace of makeup on her strong-featured face, but there was the same natural, slightly wild beauty about her that Emily had.

"Hi, Sam." Emily obviously knew the tall, balding man who stepped down from the front passenger seat. "How're things in San Diego?"

"Dry. We're still in the middle of a drought," the man said in a slow drawl, reaching out and giving Emily a hug. "You're looking good, Em."

He then turned to Laura and embraced her awkwardly, holding himself well back from her pregnant tummy and signing a clumsy "Hang loose" sign with stiff, awkward fingers.

Two other men clambered out from the back seat and were introduced by Gertrude.

"Melvin Skinner and Frank Livetti, my daughters Laura and Emily, and—hey, Kevin, come over here—this is Kevin Richardson, from Vancouver. Kevin's here taking pictures of animals and birds, and doing a little fishing, as well."

Melvin was middle-aged and paunchy, but Frank was about Kevin's age—not as tall, but dark and handsome, with regular Latin features and thick black curly hair. His wide-open smile revealed beautiful teeth. He shook hands with Laura, but when Gertrude introduced Emily, he gave her a long look and then playfully brought her fingers to his lips and made a courtly little bow over her hand.

"A wild rose," he murmured.

Emily laughed at his outrageous flattery, but it looked to Kevin as if she also enjoyed it. He wondered if Frank might like to try a ride on Spook the next morning.

Almost as an afterthought, Gertrude introduced Sam Lucas to Kevin. There was none of the polite animation in her tone when she said his name; instead, there seemed to be an awkward tension between Sam and Gertrude, and Kevin caught the knowing looks and winks that passed between Emily and Laura behind their mother's back.

Sam seemed unaffected by Gertrude's coolness. He was jovial and eager to help. Obviously, he'd been here many times before; he helped unload the truck, then shouldered his own duffel bag and marched over to one of the cabins that he apparently knew and liked. He went out of his way to help Melvin and Frank with their things, giving them the kind of tour Emily had provided for Kevin when he arrived.

"Sam seems to know his way around," Kevin remarked to Emily when they happened to arrive in the storeroom together with boxes of supplies from the truck.

Emily nodded, blowing a strand of hair out of her eyes. "Sam's been a fixture here for the past five years. He's a vet from San Diego. God knows how his practice survives all the trips he makes up here. He keeps trying to romance Ma, but she won't go for it," Emily puffed, lifting boxes of cereal to the top shelves where the mice were less likely to get into them. "Sam never gives up, though. Laura and I have stopped betting on whether he'll ever wear her down. We figure it's a lost cause. Ma's real stubborn when she wants to be."

"Sounds like Sam is, too." Kevin took a case of tins away from her and heaved them up.

"I can do that, you know." She frowned at him. "I've done this plenty of times."

"I'm sure you have." He set the last box in place and turned to face her. "But the fact is, you need more practice at allowing a guy to be chivalrous, Emily Parker." He was still annoyed over the ridiculous scene with Frank.

"As in, 'O-o-o-o-h, Kevin, you're so-o-o-o strong'?" She tipped her chin up and reached out as if to feel his biceps with a vacuous, worshipful look on her face.

His reaction was instinctive. He yanked her into his embrace and kissed her, fast and hard and thoroughly. He let her go before she had a chance to begin to struggle.

"As in, 'Me Tarzan, you Jane,'" he growled with a grin, releasing her just as Gertrude appeared in the doorway with a cooler which she plunked down on the floor.

"Is Laura still craving maple-walnut ice cream? I bought some and packed it in ice just in case. It's melting, though, so she should probably eat it quick." As she straightened, she caught a glimpse of Emily's flushed face.

"Anything wrong, honey?"

"No." Emily's response was too forceful. "No, nothing at all, Ma," she repeated in a calmer tone. "Everything's been going great." She avoided Kevin's eyes, and

the rich color that stained her cheeks rose to her hairline.

Gertrude studied her daughter for a long moment
and then gave Kevin a speculative look. He met her
piercing blue eyes with a long, challenging look of his
own. She raised her eyebrows at him, then turned on
her heel and left them. They could hear her in the
kitchen talking to the fishermen, telling a story that
made them all laugh about the hunting trip that had
bagged the moose whose head hung above the table.

"What did you do that for?" Emily hissed at him. She
seemed more flustered than angry, though. She folded
her arms across her chest and moved a step back from
him, as if anticipating that he'd do it again.

"Because I wanted to," he said in a low, urgent voice.
"Because I've wanted to kiss you again ever since that
first time out in the corral. I'm attracted to you, Emily.
It's there between us all the time. You must realize that."
He felt a sinking sensation when she didn't answer right
away. Maybe he was jumping to conclusions; maybe
the attraction he felt was one-sided.

She stared at him hard for several long heartbeats and
then expelled a long breath. "Yeah, I guess" was all she
said before she turned the way her mother had and left
him alone.

For an instant, elation filled him. She'd admitted she
was attracted to him, admitted that there was magne-
tism between them.

His heart was racing, but his mouth went suddenly
dry as the sickening knowledge flooded over him that

it was wrong of him to kiss her, worse than wrong to encourage her to admit she was drawn to him. He'd deliberately avoided it till now, but seeing Frank kissing her hand had made him a little crazy.

A *lot* crazy. After all, he was an impostor here. He was here to disrupt Emily's world, and the more he was with her, the more he realized how deep her attachment to that world really was. If she knew the whole truth about him, she'd consider his kisses insult added to injury, wouldn't she?

He was certain she would, and the knowledge tore into his gut.

He knotted a fist and slammed it hard into the wooden wall. It hurt and he swore. Then he composed his features into what he hoped was an unrevealing expression and walked out to greet the others.

Emily and Laura were putting together a late supper for the new arrivals, working in perfect tandem in the kitchen area. The others, including Gertrude, were now sprawled on the assorted couches and chairs scattered around the far end of the room. The men each had a beer, and the atmosphere was jovial and relaxed.

Emily didn't look up as Kevin went by, although he knew she saw him. He made his way over to the couch where Sam Lucas was sitting and sat down beside him.

"So this guy brought his dog in, and the poor animal was not bright...." Sam was entertaining the group with a story, but Kevin paid little attention.

"You want a beer, Kevin? They're over in that cooler on the table." Gertrude wasn't really listening to Sam's tale either, even though the vet kept glancing at her to see if he had her attention.

"You been catching any fish? Having much luck with your photos?" she queried.

Kevin told her about the fishing trips and the photo expeditions.

"I'll be taking Frank and Melvin up to Cadorna Lake tomorrow. You're welcome to come along if you want. Fishing up there's good at this time of year. What do you think? Want to join the party?"

He didn't hear the question. From the corner of his eye, he'd watched as Frank got up and wandered to the other end of the room where Emily and Laura were working. He said something Kevin couldn't hear, and Emily laughed and handed him a stack of plates. She brought silverware, and together they began to set the table, elbow to elbow, chatting steadily.

It made Kevin uneasy. Not that he was jealous, he assured himself, listening to Emily laugh again at something else Livetti said. Hell, the guy was a veritable stand-up comedian.

Jealousy had nothing to do with it. Emily didn't know this Frank character from a hole in the ground; the guy might be wanted on six counts of rape and battery, for all any of them knew. Emily should be more cautious about being overly friendly. He was surprised Gertrude wasn't more concerned.

"Sorry, what did you say?" He suddenly realized Gertrude had been talking and had now fallen silent. He turned to look at her and saw her studying him with that same piercing look she'd leveled on him in the storage room.

"I said, I'm taking the others on a fishing trip to a lake tomorrow and do you want to come along?"

He didn't. Inspiration struck. "Actually, Emily mentioned a place where I might get shots of bighorn sheep. She offered to take me up there, but we haven't made it yet."

Gertrude gave him a long look, but then she nodded. "Along Abbey Ridge, probably, and into Grizzly Camp. She wouldn't take you up there until I got here, because it would mean leaving Laura alone overnight. The mountains where the sheep are a long ways away. You'd have to pack in—it can take a couple of days to even get there, depending on weather."

Better and better.

"We'll just be making day trips, so we'll be here at night with Laura. I'll speak to Emily after dinner, if you're sure you want to make that trip. It's a tough ride, there'll still be snow up there, and there's not much as far as luxuries go. There's an old cabin, and that's about the extent of it. You'd be roughing it. Also, I don't know if Emily told you, but that's grizzly country. That's why we call the cabin Grizzly Camp. They'll be just out of hibernation now with their cubs. You'll have to pack a rifle for safety's sake. You do know how to use a rifle? And you'd also have to ford the river up at the top end."

There was another burst of laughter from Emily. Livetti was now wearing one of Laura's huge wraparound aprons, and he was helping to pour the water off of a pot of spaghetti. Emily was holding a bowl to dump it into. She was almost touching Livetti's shoulder—she was that close.

Grizzlies. Rifles. Rivers. Snow. It sounded idyllic to him. "That's just fine with me, Gertrude."

"RICHARDSON'S NOT giving you any trouble, is he, Emily? He seems to be acting a little strange around you," Gertrude commented.

The rest of the camp was asleep. Everyone had gone to bed several hours ago, but the three women had business to discuss as well as plain old gossip to catch up on, and they'd made a fresh pot of coffee and sat down at the table when the men left for the night.

"Kevin? Giving me trouble? Of course not, Ma. He's a nice guy." Emily was glad that her face was in shadow; the lantern was hanging from a nail some distance away. She was certain if her mother got a good look at her, she'd realize that "trouble" was exactly what Kevin was causing her. The problem was, she enjoyed it.

"Poor him if he tried giving Emily trouble," Laura signed. "Remember Williams?"

The three women giggled.

Brett Williams had booked several years before with Elk Valley Adventures. In his late thirties and certain that he was every woman's fantasy, he'd decided to do Emily a favor and treat her to a seduction. She overheard him telling the other three men in his party that she needed it and wanted it, and that he was just the man to give it to her.

At first she fended him off with the good humor necessary to avoid insulting a client, but one day when they were alone in camp, he became aggressive, chasing her around and refusing to believe her when she said no, even when she became furious with him.

He laughed and kept it up, convinced that she'd succumb to his charms. Emily began to believe he actually might be capable of rape.

Livid, she snatched up her rifle and leveled it at him. Still convinced it was all a joke, he came at her again.

She fired, sending a well-aimed bullet through the cabin wall just above his head, close enough to make him think she meant business. When he finally backed off, swearing at her and calling her a crazy backwoods bitch, she lost her temper completely and became the aggressor.

Holding the gun on him, she forced him down to the riverbank and made him take off everything except his fancy red bikini underpants. With the rifle as motivation, she urged him into the icy water and then made him swim around for a good long time, firing a shot or two when he tried to climb out. Every so often, she inquired sweetly as to whether or not he was cooled off yet.

It was just his bad luck that the rest of the guiding party arrived back at that moment. Gertrude and Laura knew instantly what must have happened. Without a word, Laura scooped up Brett's clothing and hustled it back to the cookshack so that when Emily did let him out of the river, he had to limp to his cabin, barefoot, nearly naked and freezing, the butt of the other men's laughter.

After dinner that night and in front of the others, Gertrude read him a lethal lecture on what would happen to vulnerable parts of his anatomy if he ever tried anything again, with either of her daughters.

After that, the women were certain Williams would leave, but they'd underestimated how cheap he was. The money he'd paid was nonrefundable, so he stayed on to the end of the contract, sullen and complaining about everything. He categorically refused to go on any excursions Emily was in charge of, so Gertrude deliberately made the trips he took with her both difficult and exhausting.

"So, you feel comfortable about taking Kevin up into Abbey Ridge?" Gertrude asked Emily. "You'll be alone with him, and you know how far that ride is. If you have any reservations, I can go instead and you can do the day trips—guide the other guys to the fishing lakes."

Emily saw Laura shake her head at their mother's suggestion. Emily's little sister was well aware of the attraction between Emily and Kevin, and she was doing her best to encourage it.

"What about poor old Sam?" Laura teased. "He'll be miserable if you go and leave him behind, Ma."

"You're a great one to talk about making men miserable, young lady. Poor Jackson called me at least seven times the last few days, worrying over you," Gertrude lectured her younger daughter. "I think you're being pigheaded about Jackson, y'know, Laura. It's not easy to raise a baby on your own, and that boy adores you and wants to marry you."

Emily rolled her eyes. She could predict exactly what her sister and mother would say next, they'd had this same conversation so often during the past months.

"Marriage between deaf and hearing won't work," Laura would declare.

"How do you know unless you try it?" Gertrude would counter.

"But Jackson can't sign properly" was Laura's next vehement line. "Communication in marriage is very important. Besides, what about you? Sam Lucas spends all his spare time here—"

"Leave Sam out of this. I'm not pregnant."

"Wow!" Laura would retort, smacking her forehead. "Big relief."

It went just as Emily knew it would, almost sign for sign. And then came her mother's grand finale, the one where Laura always laughed and Gertrude always became huffy.

"Anyhow, it looks to me as if you and Jackson have already communicated far too well," Gertrude observed with a sniff, pointing at Laura's burgeoning stomach.

Sure enough, Laura started to giggle. Then Gertrude's lips tightened and her nostrils flared.

There was one certain way to distract her mother, and Emily used it.

"Did we have enough in the bank this month to cover the loan payment and also write a check for the lease, Ma?"

The lease payment to the province on their guiding territory was already overdue by a month. The new bank manager was loath to loan them any more money; the court case had already overextended their line of credit by several thousand.

"When I deposited the checks, we had just enough to pay both, as long as nothing goes wrong on this trip," Gertrude told them. "I wrote a check for the lease just before I left and sent it by overnight mail."

Emily and Laura both heaved sighs of relief. The money problems had worried them all over the past year, but it seemed as if they were finally getting clear.

"On that cheerful note, I vote we adjourn," Emily said. "The coffeepot's empty again, and Laura's got to be up at five, right, little sister?"

Laura groaned and yawned. "Too much coffee. I should just sleep in the outhouse. You have to get up, too, Em, if you're packing into the mountains."

As she always had, Gertrude gave them each a hard good-night hug.

BY SEVEN THE NEXT morning, Emily finally had the horses packed and ready to go. Besides Cody and Lucifer, Kevin's favorite mount, they were taking a packhorse called Boney with them to carry the supplies they'd need to establish camp for a few days.

Boney's full name was Bonehead, and he'd lived up to it by being obnoxious the entire time she was trying to load him, puffing his belly out so the cinch was too loose, stepping on her toe, and threatening to bite. She was exasperated with the stupid animal by the time she and Kevin mounted and rode away from camp, and it made her short-tempered. She neck-reined Cody with one hand and with the other, held on to the long rope that controlled Boney.

Kevin, on the other hand, seemed in the best of spirits. He whistled some nameless tune as they rode along, and soon Emily began to feel more cheerful. She loved the area they were heading for. It had always been one of her favorite places—an isolated mountain meadow and lake so secluded Emily always pretended no other human knew of it except her. She felt excitement begin to grow at the thought of showing it to Kevin.

They were going to be alone up there for a while, and that added to her excitement. She looked over at Kevin, admiring him.

Most of the men who booked trips stopped shaving after the first day, and they weren't keen on bathing much, either, when they were out in the bush. But Kevin had obviously shaved that morning, and he always made good use of the bucket of hot water she delivered at daybreak.

He looked totally at home in his jeans, padded vest, worn, brown Stetson; and he controlled Lucifer with ease. Gertrude had given him a rifle and some target practice that morning while Emily was packing, and she'd told Emily that he hadn't needed any lessons on how to use the gun; he'd hit the target dead-on every time.

This city man adapted to the wilderness like a chameleon. The only remaining sign of his corporate image was the expensive digital watch on his wrist.

"I hope you're prepared for a long, hard ride today," she called to him now as they headed up the well-marked trail. There was an old seismic road here, but after a while they'd branch off at a spot called Hoffman's Draw. Beyond that point, they'd rely on Emily's knowledge of the area.

First, however, they had to ford the Elk River.

"I'm looking forward to it. Your mother said we'd have to overnight somewhere tonight."

"Yeah, at a lake called Wolverine."

"How far is it?"

"A good four hours' ride after we ford the river, but that's not too far ahead."

They didn't talk a lot, but were content instead to ride along quietly. Emily had expected problems with Boney, but to her surprise the contrary animal decided to behave like a gentleman, and ambled along behind Cody without objection.

Birds sang in constant chorus, there was just enough breeze to cool the riders down as the sun grew warmer, and a deep contentment stole over Emily as time passed without incident.

"This is where we cross the river," Emily announced at midmorning. "Boy, it still looks pretty wild, doesn't it? It's in flood, although I think it's fairly shallow. It's swift, though. There's only one place, right in the middle, where the horses will have to swim."

As they rode down the steep bank and paused on the edge, the roaring of the fast-moving water made conversation difficult.

Emily checked Boney's load over carefully, glad now that she'd spent time and energy wrapping everything in plastic and oilskin and securing it as carefully as she had on the packhorse. The river was higher than she'd expected.

At a sign from her, Kevin went in first, and she followed with the pack animal's rope held securely looped around one hand.

Ahead of her, she saw Lucifer balk a bit, but Kevin urged him in, and horse and man were soon making their careful way across the ford.

Cody was an old hand at this, and Emily gave him his head and allowed him to pick his careful way among the slippery stones under the rushing water. Boney, still surprisingly docile, followed them into the water with little urging.

Dividing her attention between Boney behind her and Kevin ahead, she watched a little anxiously as the water rose up Lucifer's flanks, sensing the moment when Kevin's mount lost his footing and was forced to swim.

In another moment, however, horse and rider were safely into shallow water again, then back on dry land. Emily felt relieved.

Kevin turned and gave her a thumbs-up sign just as Cody began swimming, and that was the very instant Boney chose to go berserk.

The pack animal, already up to his flanks in rushing water, suddenly lunged and reared at the end of his rope, pulling Emily off balance and turning Cody so that instead of being broadside to the current, he, and Emily with him, were being swept at great speed downriver.

Tilting precariously, Emily was forced to pull out of her stirrups and slide off Cody's back. But the rope from the pack animal had now become looped around her arm, and she couldn't release it.

By now, Boney had lost his footing and his meager composure entirely, and was thrashing around like a mad thing, trying to get back on dry land. The rope jerked and danced, and the current tore at Emily, whipping her underwater and then up again, making her cry out with the pain in her arm where the rope was biting into tender flesh.

Water filled her nose and lungs, and she choked, unable to see anything. She could feel the rocky bottom under her scrambling feet for tantalizing seconds, but as she struggled to get her balance, she slipped again and slid underwater. She bumped her hip hard once, and her arm scraped on the rocks as she tried frantically to grab on to something.

For one detached moment, she wondered if Emily Parker, experienced guide, was actually going to drown in the Elk River, all because of a stupid rope and a retarded packhorse.

6

"EMILY! HANG ON, I'm coming!"

Kevin spurred Lucifer back into the river.

In an instant, he'd seen the taut line between her and Boney and understood why she was being tumbled helplessly in the rushing water.

Understanding and helping were two separate things, however. Lucifer had forded the river once; he wasn't eager to try it again, and Kevin had to fight with him to get him to head back across to where the pack animal was struggling.

When he finally reached a place where he could grasp the rope, there was no way to release the tension. The packhorse was an insane whirling dervish, and Kevin wasn't able to get close enough to control him, or get enough leverage on the rope to wind it around his saddle horn and thus provide some slack at the other end. He struggled desperately for what seemed an eternity, and then, with no warning, Boney stopped his antics and clambered to his feet, head hanging, heaving and blowing water from his nostrils. Kevin lunged for the rope, almost falling off Lucifer in the process, took two quick half hitches with it on the saddle horn and moved Lucifer so that the end connected to Emily went slack.

For the first time, he was able to turn and look at her. She'd been dragged away from the deep water in the middle of the river, and was closer to the rocky shoreline where they'd begun the crossing. She was floundering, fighting to get her balance. He watched helplessly as she tried to find footing, stumbled, and fell backward once again into the shallow water. The current was strong, and it was pulling her down.

"Emily!" Frustration tore in his gut because he couldn't leave the horses to get to her to help, could do nothing except stay where he was and holler frantic directions at her. "Emily, get the rope off!"

Finally she managed to tear the rope off from her wrist and discard it, then stagger to her feet and make her unsteady way toward shore. He watched her clamber up the bank on all fours, hang her head, and vomit out the water she'd swallowed. After a time she got to her feet and tottered to a grassy knoll, collapsing in a heap as if her legs could no longer hold her.

She was safe. At least she was safe.

Until that moment, Kevin had been unaware of the utter terror that filled him, the dreadful fear that she would drown. His hands began shaking and his stomach contracted and he thought for a long moment that he, too, was going to be sick. It took an effort of will to think coherently, to try and figure out what to do next with the horses.

There was no sign of Cody, but Kevin assumed he'd probably reached the other shore; there was a bend in the river just ahead that made this seem logical. There was no point in trying to find him immediately.

Using the rope, Kevin forced Boney higher up the bank. By some miracle—and Emily's professional packing—the horse hadn't been able to totally dislodge his load. The soaking-wet burden was off center, though, and Boney listed sharply to one side when he tried to walk, but at least their supplies weren't floating down the river.

Kevin slid off Lucifer and tethered both animals securely to trees, cursing out the packhorse as he tied him. Then he ran to where Emily was slouched, her dripping head sunk down on her bent knees, her shoulders shaking.

"Emily, you okay? Jesus, Emily..."

Without thought, he knelt beside her and dragged her roughly into his arms, hugging her tightly against him, feeling the deep tremors of delayed shock that made her entire body shudder.

For a long time he just held her, soaking wet and trembling. He patted her back clumsily and stroked her dripping hair away from her face, making what he hoped were soothing sounds.

At last, she drew back a bit and looked up at him. Her eyelashes were sticking together, long and sooty against the unnatural paleness underlying the tanned skin, and her hair was plastered to her skull. A deep scratch ran down one cheek, and she winced when she moved her shoulder. The wrist where the rope had been was deeply bruised, skinned and bleeding a little.

"Thanks, Kevin. That bloody rope... It was my own fault, you know. I should have known better than to tie that blasted animal to me."

"Damn right, you should have." He shook his head, appalled at the mess she was in. "But I guess anybody can have an accident. How do you feel? Are you sure you haven't broken anything?" He reached out and touched the scratch on her face with one gentle finger.

She shook her head and stretched her legs out, trying her muscles and wincing a bit, but it didn't seem as if anything was seriously wrong.

"I swear I'm going to shoot that stupid Boney dead," she declared with a passion that made Kevin smile, reassuring him more than anything else about her condition. "This is all his fault."

He raised an eyebrow at how quickly she'd shifted blame from herself to the horse. "You might have a bit of trouble finding your rifle to do it," he said. "The last I saw of Cody, he was heading downriver at one hell of a speed."

She groaned and tried to get to her feet.

Kevin stood and helped her up, noticing for the first time a gash on her arm and another on her thigh where a gaping hole had been torn in her jeans just above her right knee. She looked down at herself and shook her head, sending droplets of water cascading over him. "Damn. These jeans were almost new, too."

"To hell with the jeans. Is there a first-aid kit in the pack somewhere?" He touched her arm gently. "We ought to get some antiseptic on these cuts. And you'd better take it easy for a while—you had a bad tumble in that river. What are my chances of finding you some dry clothes?"

She looked over at the packhorse, grazing away as if nothing had ever happened. "Boney's pack held?"

Kevin nodded.

"Hallelujah. That's about the only good luck we had, then. Our clothes and stuff ought to be quite dry. I double-wrapped everything in oilskins and then in plastic bags."

"Clever lady." He headed over to Boney and she followed. He noticed she was limping badly, and he stopped and wrapped an arm around her waist, supporting her the rest of the way.

"You hurt your leg."

She shook her head and swore under her breath. "My hip, not my leg. I think I banged into a rock. It'll be okay once I get moving."

"You banged into more than one rock, by the looks of you."

With her directing him, Kevin released Boney's pack, spread it out on the ground and located the neat bundles Emily had made of their clothing. There was a well-equipped first-aid kit. Once the plastic bags and damp oilskins were removed, the contents were totally dry. He unearthed a shirt and jeans for her, and a towel.

"What about underwear and socks?"

"I'll get them myself. Just toss me that smaller mesh bag." She was tugging off her boots and emptying the water out of them. "There ought to be a pair of runners

with my stuff, too. These are too wet to put back on."
She set the boots down and pulled off her dripping
socks. "I'll go over behind those bushes and put on this
dry stuff."

"You'll do no such thing. I'll turn my back and you
change right here."

She gave him a grateful smile. "Thanks."

"And before you pull on those dry jeans, put some
of this antiseptic cream on that gash on your leg."

She nodded. "Okay, Doc."

He turned his back to her and stared at the horses
while she struggled out of the dripping-wet clothes,
dried off roughly with the towel, and tugged on dry
garments.

Both of them were very aware that they were only a
few feet apart and she was, for several long minutes,
totally naked. Kevin could hear the small sounds she
made as she undressed, and he cursed himself for the
powerful reaction the mental image of her naked created in his body.

The lady was battered and half-drowned, for God's
sake, and all he could think of was softly rounded
curves, the tantalizing smoothness of pale skin in places
the sun hadn't touched— Hell, he had to be some kind
of pervert to be feeling this way in this particular situation.

"I'm decent, you can turn around now."

By the time he'd smoothed antiseptic cream on her
cheek and her arm, he had control of himself again.
Together they rewrapped the pack and tackled the job

of reloading Boney. They shared some of the lunch Laura had wisely wrapped in plastic—thick cheese sandwiches on whole-wheat bread that tasted fantastic. His thermos of coffee was still lukewarm, and they shared that, as well.

Kevin was relieved to see that the color was back in Emily's cheeks, and just as she'd predicted, her hip improved with use.

"I'm going to leave you here now and use Lucifer to go across and find Cody," she announced as soon as they'd finished eating. "I'll bring both horses back across and then we can try this crossing all over again."

Before she finished speaking, Kevin was shaking his head no. "The hell you are. You're not going across for Cody—I'll go. You sit down right here and rest up a bit. And don't argue with me, Emily, because it won't work."

Of course, she did anyway. "Don't be ridiculous. I'm the guide, it's my job to go. Besides, Cody doesn't know you. You won't know where to look for him—" She was making her way over to Lucifer, and Kevin stepped neatly in front of her, barring her way, hands on his hips.

"Emily, I said, don't argue," he reminded her in a low, dangerous tone. "You can easily tell me where the horse is likely to be, and I'll bring him back across."

"But—"

"No buts. I'm going, and that's that." Kevin was already untying Lucifer and climbing into the saddle. Reluctantly, she gave in, giving him directions to where she thought Cody might be. "There's a meadow down-river. He's probably grazing there."

By now, Lucifer had assumed that crossing and re-crossing the river was what was required of him, and he went into the rushing water without objecting. The crossing went smoothly, and although it took Kevin some time to locate the meadow, sure enough, Cody was there, grazing peacefully on the patches of dried grass not yet covered with snow. Kevin led the horses back to the river, and the trip back to where Emily waited was accomplished with ease.

This time they put Boney between them, with Kevin loosely holding his reins, and Emily ready to smack him from behind if he started creating a fuss. But Boney obviously had had enough excitement for one after-noon; he made the crossing like a veteran, with no problems whatsoever.

Kevin was relieved, and Emily grinned at him and gave him a thumbs-up sign as they finally clambered out of the water and onto the rocky bank. She squinted up at the sun, already long past the midpoint in the sky. The crossing had wasted valuable hours.

"We're going to have to ride hard in order to get to the overnight campsite before dark," she warned Kevin.

"Fine with me, if you're feeling up to it. Lead the way."

The ride wasn't easy. They followed a rockslide, then turned down on an invisible trail into the area Emily called Hoffman's Draw. Kevin marveled at her un-canny knowledge of the territory. He could see no markings that told her where to go or when, and yet she led the way with confidence.

They rode south through heavy bush, into a narrow valley. There were huge rocks everywhere and the horses had to be encouraged to pick their way with care. At times it was necessary to dismount and lead the animals, letting them follow carefully among the sharp boulders. The afternoon sun dropped farther toward the mountain peaks, and Emily quickened their pace whenever she could.

"Wolverine Lake, just ahead," Emily finally announced, and as they rode over a final small hill, Kevin could see a blue mountain lake nestled among trees, with a steep shale bank beyond it. The sun was setting.

"Where'll we make camp?"

"Over there, in that grove of trees. The tent frame is set up away from the lake because the wild game water there and we don't want to disturb them or change their patterns," Emily explained.

They reached the campsite and slid off their horses, both of them weary. They worked in companionable silence, unloading Boney and securing the damp tarp from his load over the wooden frame of the wall tent to make a roof for the night, rubbing the horses down and turning them loose to graze. There was a stack of firewood, and Emily started a fire and put the stew Laura had prepared for them into a pot to heat over the flames. She strung up a makeshift clothesline with a rope and draped her wet clothing over it to dry, and then set to work carefully cleaning her rifle. It hadn't gotten as wet as she'd feared, but she was meticulous nonetheless.

Later, Kevin watched but made no comment as she unwrapped the sleeping bags and laid them, one on either side on top of air mattresses, inside the walled tent.

She caught his quizzical stare and flushed. "This is grizzly country. You're going to have to share space with me tonight."

He gave her a wide, innocent smile. "Fine with me. I only hope you don't snore too loud." He ducked when she threw a towel at him, and still smiling, he grabbed the plastic bucket and took it down to the lake for water. She filled the coffeepot when he got back and set it to boil on the fire.

It was full dark by the time they ate, mopping up the succulent stew with chunks of bread, sipping mugs of the strong camp coffee, finishing with huge oatmeal cookies and tinned fruit.

The campfire made a friendly circle of light in the small clearing, but all around them was darkness and a sense of isolation, with just a hint of danger. Kevin was acutely aware that they were alone in the midst of untold miles of wilderness.

Emily seemed unaffected by the situation. She sat cross-legged, totally relaxed, elbows resting on her knees, mug cradled in both hands, staring into the campfire. He noticed, however, that her rifle was always within arm's reach.

"D'you often bring clients up here by yourself?" It was a question that had bothered him all afternoon, as they rode farther and farther into the bush. He wasn't exactly sure why it was an issue with him—he only knew it was. He tried to make his tone casual.

She nodded. "Once in a while. It depends on what they're after. I had a photographer who wanted to come up here to take pictures. And a party of fishermen, last year."

"Do you ever...?" He paused, uncertain how to phrase the question. "Have you ever had...well...had problems with the guys you guide? With them coming on to you? You're...you're an attractive woman, Emily. It would only be natural for a man to..." His voice trailed off, and, not for the first time, he cursed himself for being clumsy with words.

"It just doesn't seem too safe to me, bringing guys up here alone," he blurted. He knew he sounded like a nosy fool, but he didn't care. He'd been haunted all afternoon by images....

She turned and gave him a long, steady look. "The photographer was a sixty-year-old woman. The fishermen were all over fifty, and two of them had their wives along. You're the first man I've guided up here alone." She reached out and neatly placed another log on the fire. "I figure I can trust you." She shot him a mischievous glance. "And if I can't, there's always the rifle."

A sense of incredible relief flowed over him, mingled with a nagging uncertainty about how long he could trust himself around her. "That gun of yours is a powerful deterrent, all right."

She nodded. "Times when I *have* had problems, it's helped to have it handy," she added in a matter-of-fact way. "Guys seem to cool down real fast when they're staring down the barrel of a rifle."

He swallowed hard. "I can believe that. Have you had to use that technique often?"

She shrugged. "Once or twice."

He knew he was pushing and he didn't care. He wanted to know about her. "So, what about other guys in your life, Emily? There must have been men you cared about, that you didn't want to hold off with a gun."

It took a lot longer for her to answer this time. The campfire crackled and spat sparks, and a coyote began its eerie howling before she said, "There were a couple, over the years." She moved uncomfortably, favoring her sore hip, shifting her legs to a different position. "It never worked out. It always started out fine, but sooner or later something would come up, usually about my work." A trace of bitterness was in her voice, and her words came faster now.

"It seems hard for men to understand that this is my life, this is the work I want to do for as long as I'm able. It's not something I'm passing time at, until some knight comes along and rescues me. This valley is where I belong—it's where my roots are, it's where I'm happy and content. I'm lucky to be able to make a living doing what I love, and I have no intention of quitting and moving or changing my work just because a man thinks I should." She made a disparaging sound in her throat.

"And all of them do, you know—want me to change, to suit their lives or their concepts of what a woman should be or do. I've never met one yet who thought having a guide for a wife was a great idea."

Kevin listened, and his stomach grew sick. The fragrant coffee in his tin mug suddenly tasted like bile, and he tossed what remained into the fire.

He'd been successful, for as long as a day at a time, in forgetting what his real purpose was in being here in this valley. Emily, Laura, the complete change of daily routine, the relaxed atmosphere, the isolation itself— all had contributed to his being able to put out of his mind the knowledge of Pace Developments' imminent takeover of this entire territory . . . and the subsequent end of Emily Parker's idyllic life-style.

She was going to hate and despise him when she learned the truth. He'd known that, with some part of his brain, ever since he'd first met her.

He just hadn't known how much, and how deeply, he would care about how she felt about him.

HE COULD HEAR AN ANIMAL snuffling around just outside the tent—a small animal by the sounds it made. He wasn't able to sleep; Emily's breathing had altered subtly quite some time ago, to become the soft sighing of someone deeply asleep.

She was near enough to touch, if he stretched his hand out. A few bare boards were all that separated one air mattress from the other. He imagined her, curled inside her bag, wearing the soft blue tracksuit she'd put on instead of pajamas. He'd pulled on old track pants and a T-shirt, as well, as much for warmth as decency.

He could smell the scent of her hair mingled with the smell of woodsmoke and an underlying hint of the perfumed lotion she'd rubbed into her hands when the last of the chores were finished.

He rolled onto his back and cradled his head in his arms, aware of the thin air mattress and the hard planks under his back. He'd never slept this way with a woman before—near enough to touch and yet totally impersonal, devoid of the physical pleasures he'd always associated with sleeping with someone.

Yet sleeping this way with Emily was far more disturbing than being intimate with any of the numerous women he'd bedded over the years. Why should that be?

Her breath came in little puffs, and for a while she snored—a delicate sound that brought a smile to his lips. It was too dark to tell if she slept on her side or her back. He'd spent the long dark hours rehearsing what he'd say to her when she learned the truth about him, and every rehearsal had ended in disaster.

He turned restlessly onto his side again.

How much time did he have before he had to tell her the truth?

A week or more, maybe, depending on how long this trip lasted. And there was no point that he could see in telling her the truth before they headed back to base camp, was there?

Nope. He was going to be totally selfish here, he decided. He was going to enjoy to the fullest these few days the two of them had to spend together.

Emily was a rare woman, a unique woman. They were well on the way to becoming good friends. He wanted to know more about her, and he wanted to tell her about himself—about his childhood, his dreams. Now *that* had to be a first for him; wanting to confide in a woman. Trying to puzzle out why Emily affected him that way, he finally slipped into sleep.

SHE WAS BENDING OVER him when he awoke, and he thought for an instant maybe he was still dreaming. He reached up to her, started to say good-morning, but she put her fingers over his mouth and shook her head, making her dark hair fly, cautioning silence. Excitement made her green eyes look emerald. The scratch on her face had a scab on it. She still wore her blue track-suit and her skin was still flushed from sleep. By the faint light in the tent, it must be very early morning.

She beckoned him to come to the door, and he crawled out of his warm bag and shivered in the cold air. Emily had pushed the tent flap aside and he could see a coating of icy frost on the grass. God, it was still winter up here.

Squinting out, he saw the lake, deep blue in the gray light of dawn, and then he caught his breath with excitement.

On the steep rockslide behind the lake were two small, furry animals, balls of black fluff sliding gaily down the shale to the water's edge and scampering back up the steep incline to have another turn, playing just the way human children might on a playground slide. They looked like tiny teddy bears from this distance.

Emily handed him her binoculars.

"Baby grizzlies," she whispered close to his ear. "They're just out of hibernation, and they're trying to get rid of their itchy winter fur." She gestured to a spot on the shore of the lake, a few hundred feet from the slide. "Big Mama's right over there, keeping an eye on them. The wind's in our favor, so she hasn't smelled the horses yet, but she's a bit nervous all the same."

Kevin shifted the glasses and the mother grizzly came clearly into focus, so close he felt a shiver of apprehension raise the hairs on his neck. She was an ominous, lowering dark shape against the trees and bushes behind her. Her flat head moved from one side to the other, constantly scenting the air, and she prowled restlessly back and forth.

"My camera," Kevin groaned, remembering too late that he'd left it tucked into his saddlebag. "It's outside."

But Emily must have retrieved it, because she reached into the corner of the tent and handed it to him.

He adjusted the focus and the setting, using a zoom lens to take shot after shot of the remarkable scene. The baby grizzlies rolled and tumbled with complete abandon down their slide. The high mountain air carried their sounds clearly to Emily and Kevin, and they both laughed at their yips and squeals of joy.

Then, all at once, the mother became disturbed. She growled a low, guttural warning and hurried over to collect her cubs, batting them none too gently with a huge paw. In another moment the little family was disappearing into the woods at the north end of the lake.

Kevin lowered the camera and turned to Emily, crouching close by his side. Her face revealed her delight in sharing the spectacle of the grizzlies with him. Her eyes were sparkling, and the cold air had brought color to her cheeks.

"Worth waking up for, wouldn't you say?" she said with a wide smile.

Her rumpled tracksuit clung to her body, and in the cold air her nipples stood erect under the soft cloth.

Like the blow of a hammer, he wanted her with a sudden all-consuming need. He wanted nothing more than to gather her into his arms and wrestle them both back into the warmth of his sleeping bag while he pulled that damned blue fabric off over her head and buried his mouth in the sweet nakedness of her body.

Their gazes held, and something of what he was feeling was reflected for one long instant in her face, as well. Color flared in her cheeks. Then she moved quickly away from him, shoving her bare feet into the runners she'd positioned just inside the door.

"I'll go start the fire and make some coffee. There's cold water in that bucket—you can get washed and dressed first in here, if you like. When you're done, I'll take my turn." Her words spilled out one on top of the other and her voice wasn't quite steady. "We ought to get on the trail as soon as we can—it's still a long ride to the camp."

The tent flap closed behind her and he sat back on his haunches, eyes tightly shut as he struggled with the raging need she aroused in him.

Dear God, how was he going to survive being alone with her like this for the next few days?

He remembered his questions the night before about men coming on to her, and his face creased in a cynical grin.

Emily had better keep her rifle handy, and not because of grizzlies, either.

7

THEY HAD LUNCH IN A valley massed with flowers. Kevin had Emily name them for him.

"Curly lilies, bluebells, lily of the valley, a few late crocuses, some early wild roses, lupine, pinks and dandelions. The Indians used to pay close attention to what flowers were in bloom at what time of the year," Emily told him. "They believed their presence was an indication of what game was available, how harsh the winter would be, and how long a summer to expect." She was sprawled on her stomach on the grass—it was much drier here than it had been by Wolverine Lake, partly because of the constant wind. "This is called Windy Valley, for obvious reasons," she'd told him.

They reached Grizzly Camp late that afternoon. They'd ridden along the ridge of a mountain for several hours, and then Emily led the way down into an overgrown valley that eventually opened into a large open meadow, banked against a huge grassy slide. There was a stream flowing through the meadow, which Emily called Quarry Creek, and it emptied into a lake Kevin could see some distance away, a turquoise gem set into the green of the surrounding landscape. "Does it have a name?"

Emily nodded. "Laura named it, years ago when we were both romantic teenagers. She called it Honeymoon Lake."

Set close against the slide at the far edge of the meadow was a long, low cabin made of logs at least three feet thick. It had a flat, moss-covered roof that sloped to the back. There were shutters on all the windows and a wide overhang at the front that acted like a porch. There was a pole corral and an open-sided shelter for the horses, and an outhouse quite some distance from the cabin, facing out toward the lake.

After unpacking the horses and setting them to graze in the corral, Kevin and Emily walked over to the cabin, each carrying a load of supplies.

"Grandpa Luke built all this, and it's pretty much the same as it was years ago." Emily set her load down and wrestled with the latch on the door. "We seldom come up here, so we haven't done any renovations," she warned, finally shoving the heavy front door open.

The interior smelled musty. It was in semidarkness because of the heavy shutters, and together they propped them open on long wooden sticks. Late sunlight and fresh mountain air flooded in.

Kevin looked around curiously. The building was about forty feet long and the area where they stood was one large all-purpose room, with an old stove whose blackened chimney rose up and through the roof, a heavy, ornately carved table and some unique handmade chairs and benches. There was a makeshift sofa—

an arrangement of logs and boards and tanned animal skins.

"The bedrooms are back there—take your pick," Emily instructed.

Kevin went to examine them. There were two, taking up the width of the building with a partition between that didn't reach to the ceiling. They were cozy looking and dim because they were under the low portion of the roof, and the back of the cabin nestled against the slide. Each contained only a wide bed constructed of poles laced together with rope, supporting a wire bedspring and a burlap-covered mattress. There were a few nails on the walls to hang things on, a wooden box that acted as a bedside table, and that was all. Kevin tossed his own bags in one and laid Emily's things on the bed in the other. He found himself wishing there were only one bedroom.

"Grandpa packed the springs and mattresses in— how, I'll never know." Emily was arranging their supplies on the shelves in the kitchen area. "There's a pile of kindling out back under a lean-to. If you bring some in, I'll get the fire going and we'll have some supper. I don't know about you, but I'm famished."

Emily was never just hungry, she was *starving*, he mused. She was never just happy, she was *ecstatic*. As a result, she seemed more alive than the ordinary person. Her passion for the everyday pleasures of life fascinated him. As he loaded a box with kindling and blocks of wood, he let his mind drift, wondering how those passionate extremes would show in making love with Emily.

There'd be nothing passive about having her naked body in his arms, he was certain of that. He groaned at the physical reaction such wonderings created and set about chopping wood as therapy.

Soon there was a fire blazing in the blackened cookstove, and Emily had sliced potatoes thin and was frying them in a heavy iron skillet. Beans simmered in a pot, and bacon shared space with the potatoes after a while. The smells made Kevin's stomach rumble as he busied himself bringing in the rest of their gear. Emily wasn't the only one starving to death.

They didn't talk much during the meal; both of them ate hungrily until there was almost nothing left. Emily opened a can of peaches and they shared it for dessert, along with the last of Laura's giant cookies. Then they sat outside to watch the sun disappear over the tops of the western peaks.

"I should light the lantern and wash those dishes up." It was growing dark in the cabin, but Emily felt lethargic, pleasantly tired from the long, arduous ride.

"Why don't we wash them later? It's twilight—we could walk down to the lake. Maybe we ought to go for a swim before it gets too dark." He was improvising here. It would be great to admire Emily in a bathing suit, but also the turquoise lake did look inviting in the rosy dusk, and he was hot and sweaty from the long ride. The cabin didn't have a shower, of course.

Emily stared at him as if he'd slipped a cog. "You're nuts, Richardson, y'know that? It's May, there's snow on the ground in lots of places. I don't relish jumping in that icy water at all. I had enough of swimming in the Elk River yesterday."

"The water can't be any colder than the ocean is in Vancouver. I swim down there most of the year. Cold water doesn't bother me any," he lied. "It'll be invigorating after our long ride. Don't you feel the need of a swim to wash away all that sweat?"

She shook her head. "Definitely no."

"Hey, c'mon. We're in close quarters here. Aren't you worried about offending me with bodily odor? Besides, you're supposed to entertain me, aren't you? I'm a client, don't forget," he teased.

She shook her head at that, as well. "I plan to lock myself in the bedroom with a big basin of warm water. It's not as good as a bath, but it gets the job done."

"You mountain people are downright soft—that's your problem. All this talk about dudes and city slickers is just a cover-up for being soft."

He didn't think Emily could resist a challenge like that, and he guessed right. She gave him a narrow-eyed glare. "Find your swimming suit, hotshot," she ordered, hurrying off to get her own. "We'll see who's soft around here."

A few moments later, Kevin took a running jump and landed in the lake. For an instant, he thought he was going to have a heart attack. The water was so cold he felt paralyzed. He knew there must be chunks of ice floating somewhere close by.

Summoning up all his reserves, he forced himself to do a leisurely crawl for a few yards before turning and smiling at Emily, who stood a fair distance back from the shore, wrapped in a giant towel and eyeing him suspiciously.

"C'mon in, it's not too bad at all!" he hollered. "Refreshing." He could barely get the words past his chattering teeth, but he hoped she couldn't see that from this distance.

She did what he hoped she would, dropping her towel, mimicking his run and long, shallow dive into the lake. The instant she hit the water her breath left her in an agonized whoosh, and then she started to scream and flounder toward shore. She was out again so fast he wondered if she'd even gotten totally wet.

He wasted no time following her. Even the cool air felt warmer on his skin than the water had, and his laughter warmed him up, as well.

"That was a disgusting trick, you . . . you idiot." She flew at him and pounded him with her fists, but she was laughing now almost as hard as he was. "That damned water was freezing, and you knew it. God, I knew it would be. How did I ever let you talk me into this?"

Her one-piece red suit clung to every curve, and her body was both athletic and maddeningly sensual, just as he'd guessed it would be. Her long, wet braid swung as she lunged at him, green eyes intent on revenge. "I'm gonna pulverize you for this, Richardson."

He moved away from her to avoid the pummeling she was intent on giving him, and when she followed, he grabbed her fists and held them, immobilizing her. They were both laughing almost hysterically as she struggled to free herself.

"I'll shove you back in the water—that'll teach you," she threatened, suddenly pushing hard against him. The attack caught him unprepared, and he staggered back toward the lake before he caught himself, dragging her with him. Then, in a surprise move, he scooped her up and into his arms.

"Now we'll see who goes in," he warned, moving to the water's edge, with her kicking and screaming in his arms.

Her arms went around his neck, and she clung tightly. "If I go, so do you!" she cried.

It was intoxicating, having her in his arms, her breasts crushed against his chest. He took several menacing steps forward, but his mind was no longer on the game they were playing.

Having Emily in his arms was nothing short of marvelous. He was painfully aware of the brevity of her suit, the softness of the skin on the backs of her thighs where his forearms supported her. She was lithe and well muscled, but she was also soft. His other arm was around her ribs, and he could feel the swell of her breasts.

Her mouth was only inches from his own, and he couldn't resist any longer. He stood, legs braced, easily cradling her weight, breathing hard from both exertion and excitement.

He looked at her for a long moment, and she stilled in his arms, aware that the mood had changed.

"Emily?" It was a question, but he didn't wait for the answer. Instead, he slowly lowered his lips until they met hers in a gentle, tentative kiss.

Damn, her lips were sweet, full and lush beneath his own. He relaxed his hold on her so that she slid down his still-wet body. He steadied her when she staggered a little, but he went on kissing her, wrapping his arm around her once she was on her feet, drawing her ever closer to him, unable to resist reaching a hand up and cupping one breast. The nipple was very hard to his touch, and he could feel her breathing quicken. He was almost sick with wanting her. He slanted his head and deepened the kiss.

SOME PART OF HER had known that their roughhousing would end this way. Some part of her had invited it, chasing him as she had, playfully punching, inviting the inevitable body contact. She knew it was no proper way to go on with a client—it went against all the strict and wise rules she'd set up for herself over the years. But with this man, she'd broken those rules from the beginning, hadn't she? She knew she couldn't back away from him. Not now. Not yet.

She *wanted* him to kiss her. She'd been wanting it since the last time it happened, back in the storeroom at base camp.

What she hadn't bargained on was how the nearly naked state of their bodies would affect her—the heat and urgency of him pressed tightly against her, erect and throbbing, with only the thin nylon of their suits separating them.

His tongue was probing, searching her mouth in a sensual exploration that made her tremble, and his hand on her breast felt as though it were burning. His head tilted at a better angle, an angle designed to make his kiss still deeper. Then he groaned and released her breast as his arms came fully around her, drawing her tighter against the contours of his body, spread-eagling his legs and cupping her buttocks so she was pressed hard and intimately against his erection.

Desire filled her, heat and overwhelming need flooding into her pelvis, spreading through her entire body. A soft cry came from her throat, and her body moved instinctively against his. She knew that in another minute, they'd be on the ground, and the knowledge frightened her.

It took a superhuman effort, but she turned her head away from him, struggling to free herself.

"Stop, Kevin. Stop. Please."

For a long moment, she wondered if he would. A few more of those drugging kisses, and she knew she'd never be able to stop, either. But then he drew in a shuddering breath and allowed her to move back. He didn't release her entirely, however. His hands moved to her shoulders, holding her fast until she dared to meet his gaze. He was frowning at her.

"What is it, Emily? What's wrong?"

Her breathing was erratic and her body ached with wanting him.

It was hard to put the way she felt into words.

"You want me, I know you do." His voice was hoarse and edged with anger.

"I do. But I can't. It's . . . It's too much like a seduction," she finally blurted.

He shook his head. "I don't get it. I had the feeling you were enjoying it as much as I was. We're adults, Emily. Equals. What's this seduction nonsense, anyhow?"

She couldn't explain without revealing more of herself than she cared to right now. Instead, she shrugged his hands off her shoulders, located her thongs and shoved her feet into them, then found her towel and wrapped it protectively around her as she started back across the meadow to the cabin.

He didn't follow her immediately, and she was grateful for that. She lit the lantern and got dressed in jeans and a warm shirt. Then she revived the dying fire in the stove, put water on to heat for dishes and set to work clearing away the remains of their supper.

It was dark by the time he came in. He had a shirt slung over his swim trunks, and she couldn't stop herself from glancing at his well-muscled body when she thought he wasn't looking. She'd seen him in running shorts, so she knew what he looked like, but she couldn't help herself. He had beautiful legs, long and strong, and the rest of him was perfectly proportioned.

She wondered if he was furious with her for running off like that.

But he grinned at her cheerfully and remarked, "I suppose you know there's no door on that outhouse."

Relief flooded her, and she smiled at him. "Grandpa believed in being able to admire the view. He positioned it so that it's facing away from the cabin, looking out on the lake and the mountains."

"Takes a bit of getting used to for those of us from the city. Give me a minute to get my jeans on and I'll dry those dishes for you."

So she washed and he dried, carefully and methodically, handling the sturdy plastic plates and tin cups as though they were the finest china. His hands were big, but long and graceful rather than clumsy. She shivered, thinking of them on her body.

"You want to tell me what that was all about out there, Emily?"

She scrubbed the bean pot with more energy than it really required.

He was drying cutlery, and he went on sorting spoons and knives into their proper places in the drawer.

"What I said about seduction?" She cleared her throat unnecessarily and blundered on: "Men sometimes come here to the valley, find out I'm their guide, and decide that it might be fun to get me into bed with them. That it would make a great hunting story to tell their friends back in the city, about the hot little backwoods woman they got it on with when they were fishing. Which wouldn't matter at all if I had the same attitude they had toward sex. Casual fun, great exercise, notches in the belt and all that. But I don't—feel that way at all about sex." Her face was hot. "So it makes me really nervous about having anything to do with clients—in a sexual sense." She stared down at the heavy pot, scrubbing it even though there wasn't a scrap of anything left in it.

He didn't answer for a long time, and while she waited, she decided she'd botched this one really good, damn it all to hell.

At last he reached out and took the pot from her. "Is that what you figure I'm doing, Emily? Trying to score with you as some kind of ego boost, a notch in my belt?" His tone was neutral, and she shot him a sidelong glance to see if any emotion showed in his face. It didn't. "I told you once before, that isn't how I operate."

Frustrated, she threw the dishcloth into the basin of water, and it sloshed all over her shirt. "Goddamn, now I'm all wet again. How the hell do I know what you're trying to do, Richardson? I've only known you a week, that doesn't qualify for in-depth psychoanalysis. I just know it's a big mistake to start trusting men, especially ones I guide in the bush." She dabbed at her shirt with a towel. This whole thing was getting worse and worse.

"Sounds to me like some guy hurt you pretty bad." His voice was still neutral, but when she glanced at him, he was looking at her intently. "That right, Emily?"

She opened her mouth to deny it and heard herself agreeing instead. "Yeah. I guess so."

Kevin filled two mugs with coffee from the pot on the stove, fixing hers the way she liked it with one sugar and a dab of tinned milk. He took them over to the sofa and sat down, patting the bear hide in silent invitation. After a moment, she dried her hands and plunked down beside him, accepting the coffee mug.

"You feel like talking about it?" He made it sound as if it wouldn't matter even if she didn't.

She shrugged and sipped her coffee. "There's not much to tell—it was a long time ago." She concentrated on keeping her voice light and easy, as if the story were just that—a story. "I was young and naive, in my early twenties. We had this party from Texas—a couple of lawyers, two ranchers, and this cowboy, Jake Fowler. He was so polite, Jake, such a gentleman, and yet he knew his way around in the bush. He wasn't any tenderfoot, and that impressed me. The rest of the party were after bear, but he wanted to fish, so I ended up spending quite a bit of time alone with him. I wasn't exactly a woman of the world in those days, and he knew exactly how to make me feel special." She knew she sounded bitter, but she couldn't help it.

"You can probably guess the rest. I was such a gullible kid. I fell for him hard, and things got…involved. He made all sorts of promises about a future together, telling me how he'd fallen deeply in love with me. I believed him." She took a long sip of her coffee before she went on, and Kevin waited without saying anything. She had to clear her throat before she could continue. "Then I overheard him the night before they all were due to leave, telling his buddies what a stud he was and how he had little old Emily just panting for him, wrapped around his finger. They were all drinking and having a good old laugh at my expense."

Kevin's voice had a hard edge. "What did you do?"

She made a sound intended as a laugh. "Nothing. Not a single thing. I felt humiliated and utterly ashamed for being so gullible. I was too young, too naive, to confront him the way I would now. I took off like a scalded cat, packed off alone into the bush at daybreak the next day and stayed away a week, so I never saw him again."

"And now you're judging me by Jake Fowler." It was a statement more than a question, and it irritated Emily.

"Don't be ridiculous, of course I'm not. I'm not that stupid. It's just that I made up my mind after that experience that I'd never be impulsive again. I'd take my time with romance, think everything through thoroughly before I committed myself to anyone in any way. And I also decided to make sure business stayed business with clients."

"And you've stuck to that?"

"Yeah." She nodded, still not daring to look at him. "Pretty much. It's never really been a big issue, because there haven't exactly been hordes of men I was interested in. Or the other way around, come to think of it." There was wry humor in her tone that tore at his heart. "Most of the clients we get aren't really hard to say no to, and like I told you before, the local guys don't stick around long when they find out I spend a fair amount of my life up in the bush and intend to go on doing so."

He was quiet for a long time. His thoughts were confused. He wondered just exactly where Jake Fowler might be by now, and he indulged in fantasies of meeting him. He thought about Emily—how complex she was, and also how direct and honest.

At last he said, "So where does that leave us, Emily? You and me?"

She wouldn't look at him. She got up and put her cup on the rough wooden counter. He was a client, and she ought to simply remind him again that she didn't go to bed with clients. Except that she knew her rule wasn't going to hold up in this case; she'd known it when she agreed to bring him here to Grizzly Camp.

She wanted him to make love to her, but her pride insisted that she be the one to choose the moment. It couldn't just happen, willy-nilly, as if it were accidental. It was too important to her, although she didn't think about why that was.

Instead, she looked over at him, meeting his eyes and holding the contact as she told him honestly, "I need some time, Kevin. I'll know when the time is right."

He gave her that lopsided grin and nodded without saying anything more.

They went to bed shortly afterward, one on each side of the thin partition. As she'd said she would, Emily took a basin of warm water into her bedroom and sponge-bathed before she pulled on her warm tracksuit, poignantly aware of her nakedness and Kevin only yards away. The last sound she heard before sleep overcame her was Kevin's voice.

"'Night, Emily," he said softly. "Sweet dreams, sweetheart."

HE CAME OUT OF A DEEP sleep with the feeling that he wasn't alone in the room. It was still full dark; the window was only a shade lighter than the blackness inside. He'd propped the window open, and a cool breeze filtered across his face and arms as he jerked up on one elbow, squinting to see into the shadows. His sleep-drugged mind produced images of bears breaking into the cabin . . . porcupines . . . cougars. . . .

"You awake, Kevin?" Emily's whisper was so soft and husky he barely made out the words.

"Yeah. What's wrong? What is it?" He struggled to get up, but the sleeping bag held him fast and he cursed under his breath, remembering that his rifle was at the foot of the bed, propped against a chair.

She was closer to the bed when she answered, but she still whispered. "Nothing's wrong." There was a pause, and then in an even softer murmur she said, "If it's all right with you, I think I've had enough time now, Kevin."

His heart thumped like a sledgehammer against his chest wall and he had to swallow hard. "Come here, love," he managed to growl, and an instant later he had her in his arms and in his sleeping bag.

She was naked, and the shock of having her—satin smooth and quivering in his arms—brought a surge of desire so powerful he thought he might explode just from touching her.

8

SHE WAS TREMBLING, and he wasn't sure if it was from nerves or chill. The room was cold, and he settled them inside his narrow sleeping bag, supporting her head on one arm, drunk with the delight of having her bare body pressed tightly to his.

"I want this, Kevin, but there have to be some rules." Emily pulled away a little. "While we're up here, we'll just pretend that we're a man and a woman, alone together, suffering from...from some exotic kind of valley fever. But when the time up here is over, so is...is this. I don't want either of us thinking there's a future, because of course, there isn't."

It was important to her that he didn't think for one moment she was projecting a future based on this, or making any demands whatsoever on him. Her pride insisted they get it straight in the beginning. "So when we get back to base camp, we're guide and client again, as if this had never happened, right? We have to be really clear about it, before we...we start. Agreed?"

He'd have agreed to anything, just to keep her in his arms.

"I suppose it's for the best, if that's the way you want it," he said, wondering how he'd ever be able to pretend he hadn't held her, loved her.

But he could tell by the conviction in her voice that her mind was made up, and he knew her well enough to know she'd leave him now if he argued—and this moment might never come again.

He had no intention of arguing.

"Emily...Em. Oh, God, you're beautiful." He stroked her, holding back his own overwhelming urge to hurry, calming her, helping her relax. He touched her full breast, delighting at the weight of it in his hand, cupping it and teasing the hard bud of her nipple with his thumb, feeling himself surge dangerously as she moaned and moved her hips against him.

"Easy, love. Slow and easy. We've got all night."

All night, all day, all the next night, the week ahead, alone with her, seemed to expand into delicious eternity. He felt drunk with delight.

He kissed her, slowly and deeply and thoroughly, thrilling to the way her tongue answered his. He slid a hand down her body, exploring luscious curves, learning what areas were most sensitive to his touch. At last his fingers found the cleft between her legs and she cried out and moved against his hand as he rubbed her there.

He whispered to her, telling her all the things he'd dreamed of doing during the long nights since he'd met her.

"I want you now, Kevin." The words were a soft breath in his ear.

Their bodies were damp now with perspiration, and he shoved the encumbering bag down until they lay naked on the sheet. With a whispered apology, he left her for a moment, fumbling in the pack he'd left on the floor beside his pants for the small, foil-wrapped package that would protect her.

Then she was in his arms again, and this time he straddled her, letting his body cover hers.

"Is this all right, love? I'm not too heavy on you?"

She didn't answer in words—he drew in a shuddering breath as her hand moved down between them and closed around his penis, guiding it into her.

EMILY FELT his penis slowly penetrate her, and she wrapped her legs around him, raising herself to meet his rhythm. The power of her feelings—the depth of her wanting something entirely new in her admittedly limited experience—took her by surprise.

Small gasps of pleasure became sounds of urgency she couldn't suppress. She writhed beneath him, lost to everything except the terrible concentrated ache low in her belly and her desperate need for the man who held her clasped tightly in his arms. He whispered encouragement and moved in a maddening cadence that intensified the pleasure scalding through her. The sounds she made grew louder and more urgent. She moved her hands over his back and buttocks, urging him on, willing him to hurry.

She sobbed his name, and as he moved into her with a powerful thrust, her body convulsed, every muscle contracting as her entire being erupted into ecstasy.

When Kevin began to climax, a guttural shout erupted from his throat. The pleasure went on and on, leaving him drained and replete.

After a time he shifted so his weight wasn't full on Emily. She lay in his arms, her breathing slow and languorous.

"Emily?" He reached down and pulled the sleeping bag up, unzipping it so it made a blanket over them. Carefully, he covered her bare shoulders, folding himself around her so they lay like spoons under the eiderdown bag, his front curled snugly around her back.

"Em, are you okay?"

Her voice was thick with sleep already, and he grinned at her slightly aggrieved tone. "Of course I'm okay. Don't talk. I feel too nice to talk. Go to sleep, Richardson."

Within minutes, he had.

HE KNEW BY THE FAINT light coming through the window that it was still very early. But not too early for Emily. She was already up and evidently long gone. He wondered if she was in the outer room, stoking the fire, but there was no sound except bird noises from outside.

Suddenly he grew anxious, concerned that perhaps she was regretting what had happened in the night.

Yet how could she regret something that fantastic? He marveled at the power of what had passed between them. She was a magnificent, fiery woman, more passionate than he'd imagined a woman could be. She was earthy and honest and lovely. Just thinking about her, he wanted her again.

He paused in the act of pulling on his pants.

And you, Richardson, are a lying son of a bitch. You know that, don't you?

He sat back down on the bed, immobilized by overwhelming guilt. More than anything in the world, he wanted Emily to respect him, to believe in him, to be his lover and his friend. He was drawn to her in a way he'd never been to a woman. For the first time in his life, he wanted to be with her, alone with her, for as long as fate would allow.

Which wouldn't be long at all.

A week, if he was lucky, and then Pace Developments and all it represented would ruin everything. The sick feeling in his gut intensified.

Take each day one at a time, or you'll ruin what could be a little shot at wonderful.

He yanked his pants up and zipped them, then grabbed a flannel shirt.

He needed to see her. He needed to make sure things were okay between them. He needed to make love to her again.

He'd live for the moment, and let tomorrow take care of itself. For as long as he could.

EMILY HAD AWOKEN when dawn was about to break. She'd slid out of his arms, allowing herself to feast her eyes on Kevin's sleeping face, his rumpled hair, and the strong, muscular shoulders that protruded from the opened sleeping bag.

He looked so vulnerable lying there. Innocent, even. Memories of the night came flooding into her head, and her cheeks burned.

He wasn't innocent at all. He was a forceful, accomplished lover, far more experienced than she was. He'd drawn depths of passionate response from her that astounded her when she remembered their lovemaking. Was that his technique, or was it something in her—a response she'd never experienced before with a man?

She didn't want to think too much about that, so she crept out of the bedroom, shutting the door quietly behind her. She shivered as she used the icy water in the basin to wash herself. Then she pulled on her jeans and a heavy red checkered shirt. She ran a brush through her hair, leaving it loose, then laid a fire in the cookstove and lit it.

Outside, the sun was rising over mountain peaks that reflected its gold and fiery pink. The lake mirrored the glory of the sky, and the meadow shone as if diamonds were scattered there as the early light caught the dew. It was perfectly still, and the high mountain air was invigorating and pure.

Emily caught her breath in appreciation. She stood in front of the cabin and slowly turned in a full circle, arms spread wide and welcoming, greeting the morning. Then she grabbed a pail and went down to the creek, bending to scoop up a bucket of the clear, icy-cold water.

A great contentment overcame her as she walked back toward the cabin, swinging the pail easily. This camp was where she felt most at home, this was the place she treasured above all others in what she thought of as "her valley." There was something here that brought her both happiness and peace.

Kevin was coming toward her across the meadow, moving in that athletic manner she'd come to associate with him. She watched him, remembering how it felt to touch his naked chest, his back, his buttocks. No single part of him was strange to her now.

He didn't say anything until he was very close to her.

"You look like a pagan goddess, swinging across the grass with your hair loose like that." His voice was deep and husky, and his smile tender.

She was about to joke about goddesses not wearing jeans and shirts, but then she looked into his eyes and saw how much he meant it, and joy filled her heart. She grinned at him, and he reached out and took the water pail from her and set it on the ground. Then he gathered her into his arms, burying his face in her hair, pressing kisses on her neck, her chin, the tip of her nose, making her giggle.

"You're my wild, beautiful woman," he growled, scooping her up and into his arms.

Emily wrapped her arms around his neck. "Kevin, put me down. You're going to put your back out, carrying me around all the time...."

But he was laughing down at her and shaking his head, striding toward the cabin as if she weighed no more than the bucket of water abandoned on the grass behind them.

"The fire—we have to put wood on the fire...."

"Forget the fire. I know this great way to keep warm." He walked with her straight through to his bedroom and dumped her on the bed.

"Now," he said, kneeling over her and beginning to unbutton the red shirt. "Last night was fabulous, my pagan lady, but it was also a cheat because I couldn't look at you. We'll take our time, and I can kiss each part of you, here...." He spread the shirt open and gently cupped each of her naked breasts in his hands. He leaned forward and took one nipple and then the other into his mouth, suckling her until she cried out and moved sinuously beneath him. The movement of his hot, wet lips and tongue on her nipples started a blaze inside her. Swiftly he stripped off her jeans and the cotton panties she wore under them, and his hands stroked her body, making her quiver.

"You, too," she told him. "No fair, me being naked alone." Her voice was unsteady but her fingers were nimble as she undid the buttons on his shirt.

Within seconds, they were both nude. Far from the leisurely love dance he'd envisioned, they came together with the same wild and desperate passion they'd shared the night before, except that this time Emily struggled out from under him. She settled herself astride him, taking his penis inside her.

Her head fell back, her silky dark hair spilling over her shoulders, her glorious body unashamedly displayed to him as she rocked them both swiftly to completion, collapsing on his chest when it was over.

He held her until their breathing slowly became normal.

"I read somewhere that making love should take hours," he said, threading his fingers through her hair. "I think we need a lot of practice at this."

"We could always set a timer," she agreed in a sleepy, contented voice. "Although for us, this fast way is lots better."

"Why's that?"

"Because," she said matter-of-factly, struggling out of his arms and trying to find the panties he'd tossed carelessly away, "you and I don't have the luxury of time."

He felt a weight shift and settle in his chest as he watched her.

"We have this week, all alone together here," he reminded her and himself.

"That's what I mean. That's not a whole lot of time. Now get up, lazybones, and help me make us some breakfast. By now that fire's gone out and we'll have to start it all over again."

He lunged at her playfully and tumbled her back on the bed. "Fine with me," he leered in his best lecherous voice. "I can probably start another fire, given an hour or so and some potent vitamins. You've ruined me, woman."

They collapsed together, laughing, but it took only a few moments for his body to signal his readiness. And this time, their loving was as slow as he'd envisioned it could be. This time, the game was his. He deliberately brought her near to the heights of passion and then held back, until they both were delirious with need. When they could wait no longer, locked as one, they climaxed rapturously.

It was long past noon when they finally got the stove going. Emily fried bacon and eggs and made hot biscuits, and they devoured every scrap.

"This time, I really was starving to death," she declared, swallowing the last morsel of biscuit smothered in strawberry preserves. "Now we can wash up these dishes and then go out picture hunting." She sprang to her feet and began energetically scraping plates and filling the dish basin.

"I was thinking more along the lines of another little nap," he countered hopefully.

Emily pretended to be scandalized. "You're a sex fiend. I'm stranded a hundred miles from nowhere with a sex maniac."

"I hate to disappoint you, but I mean a nap, nap. As in two or three hours of sleep." There was a poignant, hopeful note in his voice. "I'm feeling just a little bit weary."

"Nope. Sorry. You just shouldn't have eaten so much." Emily sloshed the dishes in and out of the water and layered them carelessly on a towel to drip-dry. "The agreement was, you would be exposed to all manner of wildlife, and that's exactly what we're going to do."

"But I've already experienced all the wildlife I can handle for one day," he said, and she couldn't help laughing with him. But she didn't relent, either.

"On your feet, Richardson. We're going to ride up the meadow and then hike up Abbey Ridge and see if we can find you any mountain goats to photograph. Or moose, or deer, or something."

"I can't move. I'm incapacitated. Maybe a kiss would help." For all his complaints about not having energy, he got up and moved toward her, a crooked grin on his face.

She put a chair between them. "Stop. That's close enough. I don't trust you." Holding him at arm's length, she bent forward and planted a kiss on his lips. "There you go. Now, just shoulder this pack, get your rifle, and head out the door."

With one quick movement, the chair was pushed aside and she was pulled into his arms and he was kissing her thoroughly. When the last shred of her resistance was gone, he released her.

In a kind of mutual rapturous stupor, they took up their gear and headed out to saddle the horses.

LATER, HE REMEMBERED that long afternoon not so much for the astonishing variety of wild animals they encountered, but rather for the depth of communication between them. It seemed as if their physical joining had made it possible to be entirely open with each other—at least, about some things.

Kevin still didn't mention Pace Developments, but for the first time he could remember, he was able to talk about his mother.

On horseback, they ambled past the lake and headed up the long meadow.

"Look, there's a cow moose with her calf." Emily's voice was filled with excitement.

The huge, lumbering animal hadn't scented them. She was up to her knees in a swampy bog, devouring some form of vegetation with her gangly calf close beside her, doing his best to imitate his mother.

"He's adorable, isn't he?" Emily was smiling, eyes shining at the scene, but she deliberately kept some distance between them and the moose. "A cow with a calf can be dangerous," she warned Kevin. "Be ready to run if we need to."

Kevin snapped several frames before the cow scented them. Then she hurried off into the woods, nosing her calf ahead of her.

"I love the springtime, when all the animal mothers have their new babies. It always touches me, what good care they take of their offspring. They sure don't get any help from Papa. He does his biological bit, and then disappears, so the whole rearing process is up to the mother." She was quiet for a moment, then added, "Not so different from the way I was raised, come to think of it. My dad wasn't the strong one in our household even when he was alive. Him and Ma fought a lot. I've often thought that if he hadn't died, they might have divorced anyway. Either way, I guess it would have been Ma who raised us."

"Your mother raised you, my father raised me," Kevin heard himself say. "I never knew my mother at all."

Emily was silent. She remembered once before, asking him about his mother and having him clam up for hours. She wasn't going to make that mistake a second time. But to her surprise, he went on explaining this time.

"She had a nervous breakdown after I was born." His voice was cool and controlled, as if what he was talking about didn't really concern him at all. "These days I guess they call it postpartum depression. Anyhow, it got worse instead of better, and finally she was hospitalized when I was about two. It took eight years for her to recover to the point where she could leave the sanitarium, and when she finally did, she never did come back to live with my father. Instead, she divorced him and immediately married an Englishman, someone she'd met while she was ill. She went to live in London. She died five years ago."

The story said so much about Kevin, about the lonely little boy he must have been. It tore at her heart. She wanted—needed—to know more. Large parts of the story were still missing. Emily couldn't hold back her questions.

"But didn't you visit her while she was ill? It must have been terrible for her, and for you, too, not being around while you were growing up."

He shrugged. "I never really got to know her at all. Dad didn't think it was right to take me to the sanitarium she was in, so I only saw her a half-dozen times in all those years. When she got out, she had me visit her a couple of times, but by then, we were strangers. She wasn't comfortable with me, and when she got married and left the country, Dad wouldn't let me go visit her. I guess she never pushed him much for visitation rights. By the time I was old enough to go on my own, I just couldn't do it. She was a stranger. I felt as though I'd be intruding in her life."

Emily was horrified and saddened by the story. Her own relationship with Gertrude was so close it was almost impossible for her to imagine the situation Kevin described.

"Did . . . did you go to her funeral?"

Kevin shook his head. "I was in Montana scouting out some land when it happened, and by the time they located me, it was too late to go over. Besides, it seemed kind of crazy. I'd never gone when she was alive, so it seemed hypocritical to me to fly over after she'd died."

There was defensiveness in his tone, and Emily recognized it. He felt guilty, and her heart went out to him. "I understand perfectly," she reassured him, and was rewarded by the look he gave her. But there was more she needed to know about him, now that he was willing to tell her.

"So I guess you're really close to your dad, huh?"

There was a long silence before he answered, and this time his voice had a hard edge. "Not really, no. Not at all, in fact. I had a live-in baby-sitter before I was sent off to boarding school. That happened at five. In summer he paid for me to go to different camps, I guess to keep me out of his hair. See, my father is dedicated to his business. I guess you'd call him a workaholic, and it wasn't until I was grown and went to work for him that I got to know him at all. We're good business partners—" there was tension and uncertainty in his voice "—but you couldn't really say we have much of a father-son relationship. We never had."

"God, Kevin." Emily couldn't hide her dismay. "That doesn't sound like much of a childhood to me. You got cheated." It sounded totally dismal, in fact, and she felt a wave of gratitude for her own unconventional yet loving upbringing. "But your father must want more of a relationship than what you describe. After all, you're his son. Haven't you ever tried to talk to him about it?"

Kevin laughed—a bark of sound that wasn't laughter at all. "You don't know my father. Barney would run a mile to get away from a conversation like that. And I wouldn't have the first clue how to go about it. We never discuss things like father-son relationships."

Emily was appalled. "Well, maybe you ought to start. I mean, he won't be around forever, and he's the only parent you've got. I wish lots of times that my dad had lived longer, so I could have talked with him more.

Anyhow, it's no wonder you didn't want to talk much about your mother. You must feel pretty angry with her, cutting you out of her life that way. I sure would. I was good and mad at my dad for years, for dying on us the way he did."

He shot her a quizzical look. "Angry with my mother? I never thought of it that way. I guess as a kid I used to feel mad at her sometimes—more hurt than mad, actually. But once I grew up I realized that my father wasn't very good husband material, and that probably the way he was ... is ... had a lot to do with her psychological problems. He wouldn't be the easiest guy in the world to live with, believe me." He gave a short, harsh laugh. "But then, my ex-wife Donna made it clear that I wasn't any prize in that department, either."

"Why's that?"

He grinned at her again, and this time it was rueful and open. "I paid more attention to sporting events and business than I did to her, and you may have noticed that I'm not that hot at conversation."

"You seem to be doing okay to me." She winked at him, trying to lighten the atmosphere. "You've improved drastically the past few days."

"It must be this air or something. Normally, I don't say a whole lot. I was never good with words—I was always better at sports than I was at debating."

Her voice was very careful now. "So you figure the marriage breakup was all your fault?"

He nodded. "Absolutely. It took me a few years to see it, but I eventually realized that Donna was right about me. I'm a poor risk for matrimony, all right."

Something inside her wanted to argue with him, but she resisted. "Well, that makes two of us. I've never really wanted to get married, and at my age, the chances of ever getting into it decline sharply anyhow. So I figure I'll end up the local eccentric, that batty old bachelor woman who lives up at Abbey Ridge and threatens to shoot anybody who trespasses on Grizzly Camp."

"Anybody?" He gave her a teasing look. "Wouldn't you make an exception for some tenderfoot who saved you from drowning in the Elk River, and then used extraordinary measures to keep you warm at night? Somebody who follows you faithfully up shale mountainsides without complaining, when he'd rather be doing . . . other things?"

"Can it, Richardson." Her cheeks flushed and she shot him a sidelong glance. "Well, I might at that. You never know your luck." She changed the subject. "This is where we leave the horses and start up the mountain on foot. Be sure to take your camera and your rifle—there's a lot of grizzlies around here."

He looked at the steep, rocky incline. Grizzlies, and a nearly perpendicular climb for God knows how far.

"You have no idea how excited I am about this, Emily," he muttered under his breath. "How long do you figure it'll take us?" he asked aloud.

"Oh, two hours up, another hour or so to come down. It's great exercise, and we've got all afternoon."

He gave her a narrow-eyed look. "If it's exercise you wanted, we could have stayed back at the cabin."

She just grinned mischievously at him and led the way up the slope.

9

IT TOOK FOUR DAYS for Kevin to realize he'd stopped wearing his watch. Time, always metered out by him in meticulous units and spent with miserly care, became a matter of simple rhythms.

He and Emily slept when they were tired, awoke when they felt rested, ate when hunger demanded it, and made love whenever it suited them—which turned out to be far more often than either of them had ever dreamed possible. They also talked and laughed and argued, and even fought over issues they felt strongly enough about—or issues they didn't feel strongly about at all, like Emily's total lack of interest in political matters.

Kevin found out she didn't even bother voting half the time, and he was shocked. Emily laughed at him and insisted it was her constitutional right to vote or not, just as she chose, and they ended up in a shouting match over it. She threw a tin cup at him and hit him on the ear.

They made up in the very best possible way, of course.

"KEVIN, IS IT LIKE THIS often, between men and women?" It was late afternoon, and they'd taken a picnic to the shore of the lake. Summer seemed to have happened without a spring interval. The air was calm, and the sun hot. They'd swum in the icy water, eaten lounging on a blanket spread on the grass, and then they'd made love, slowly and languorously.

Her head was on his chest, and she could feel his heartbeat and his breathing. His eyes were closed, but she knew he wasn't sleeping.

She'd reached a stage with him where she felt she could ask him anything at all, and he'd do his best to answer. They'd formed a bond that made her feel safe and cherished and free.

"Kevin? Talk to me. Is this usual?"

He opened his eyes and looked at her, his gaze questioning. "You should be able to answer that for yourself."

She flushed and stammered a bit. "Well, it isn't as if I've had that much experience. Not as much as you, anyhow. You were married, after all, and you're a single man living in a big city, and I just wondered if . . . if this is how it's supposed to be," she finished lamely, "all the time."

What could he tell her?

Kevin studied Emily—the high cheekbones, the sunburned nose that was peeling a little, the clear green eyes with their long dark lashes. His arms were around her, and her voluptuous body lay bare to his gaze, with only the thin cotton shirt she'd pulled on as protection from the sun half covering her breasts.

Emily was as unspoiled and primitively beautiful as this valley she loved. She was unique. He'd never known a woman like her—so openly sensual and yet so innocent in some curious way. She was forthright in her speech and manner, and with her he found he could reveal himself more honestly than he usually could. But this question was tough. He struggled with an answer: "Everyone's different, I guess. No two people react the same way to any two other people—you know that." He stroked his thumb down the skin of her throat, marveling at its softness. "But what we have here is pretty unusual, I think. For one thing, I've never made love to a good friend before."

"Me, neither. Maybe that's what makes the difference—that we're friends."

"Yeah," he agreed, not believing it at all. There was a magic with Emily that went far beyond friendship. "We're also in a unique situation here. There're no distractions whatsoever, except for that battery-operated telephone you have to crank up, no television, or other people dropping by. It's the perfect setting, sort of our own Garden of Eden."

She giggled. "Without the snake. At least, I don't think there's snakes up here. But there's every other form of wildlife, so maybe I just haven't met any yet."

A familiar knot formed in his stomach. There was a snake, all right.

She sighed deeply. "Anyhow, this week's been about the best time of my whole life, but we're going to have to think about heading out pretty soon. We've already been here two days longer than I'd planned. You're going to be overdue, getting back to Vancouver."

"A couple more days can't hurt—they won't send out a search party for me quite yet," he reassured in a husky voice, kissing her ear.

"Where do you live in Vancouver, Kev?"

"In an apartment, out near the university area."

"Is it a nice place—homey? Do you have a yard?"

"Nope, it's on the twelfth floor. It does have a tiny balcony and a view of Spanish Banks, but that's about it. I'm not much of a homemaker, and anyhow, I don't spend a lot of time there."

Vancouver seemed very far away, and he fantasized for a moment about what it would be like never to have to go back.

THE REALIZATION THAT their time alone together was fast drawing to a close woke him in the middle of that night. It was black dark, with no sign yet of dawn. Emily was cuddled close to his side. His arm rested protectively across her, her breast cupped in his hand, her firm buttocks curled into his belly.

She was deeply asleep, snoring just a little. It made him smile, because she got quite huffy and insulted when he teased her about snoring.

He'd managed not to think too much or too often during the past several days about the way he was deceiving Emily. Instead, he'd abandoned himself totally to the pleasure of being with her. He'd never shared thoughts, dreams and memories with anyone the way he did with her.

He'd found himself awed and fascinated by the day trips she took him on. Emily had made him a gift of her valley, taking him places she openly admitted she'd never taken anyone before. It became very clear to him that the valley was not just a place where she made her living, but more important, the place where heart and soul were at home.

During their excursions, he'd tried to discuss their relationship with her, wanting to let her know that it was special to him, but she wouldn't listen.

"We had an agreement—this week and that's all, valley fever and no regrets. Let's stick to it, okay?"

No regrets. What a joke that was. His mind went from Emily inevitably to Pace, and his father. Kevin had decided to lie to Barney, telling him that the area wasn't what they'd hoped it might be, in a last-ditch effort to protect the Parker women.

But he knew it was a fruitless endeavor. Barney had already set the wheels in motion, and there was nothing Kevin could do about it.

There was one thing, he corrected himself, feeling the bile rise in his throat: He could tell Emily before they left here. He could confess to her and try to make her understand that he'd cancel the entire plan if he could, that he despised himself for misleading her about who and what he was. And he was sorry, so terribly sorry, for what his company planned to do.

He could do that—throw himself at her mercy and beg her forgiveness for ruining her life. And where would it get him? Worse still, it would spoil the magic of this place for both of them, forever. Instead of memories of a few days spent in paradise, this camp would be forever tainted in both their minds with the echoes of the inevitable quarrel and the awful ramifications of his confession.

Nope. He'd rather wait until they got back to base camp, he decided.

He'd tell Emily first, alone, and then he'd have to confess to the other two Parker women, as well. The prospect was horrifying, but he made up his mind that it was the only honorable thing left to him.

Emily sighed and snuggled against him as rain began to patter on the roof overhead. Kevin settled her as close to him as he could, covering her one bare shoulder and wishing time would simply stop, that they could stay in their mountain cabin forever.

He lay still, holding her, and waiting for daybreak.

SINCE THEIR ARRIVAL, Emily had used the battery-operated phone several times to make contact with base camp and assure Gertrude of their safety. That afternoon she used it again, and when she hung up, worry was evident on her face.

"Ma says it's raining pretty hard down there, and that the river's up. She got a weather report and there's a heavy storm passing through, to last maybe a week or more. We don't have enough supplies to sit that out up here, even if you had the time. Which you don't. Right?"

Kevin's trip was officially over. He knew if he stayed much longer, Barney would find a way to contact him to see what the problem was, and he'd rather not have his father talking to Gertrude before he'd had a chance to talk to her himself.

"Right," he confirmed with reluctance.

"Well, we'd better pack up tonight and leave early tomorrow for base camp. Ma thinks we'll have to ride out the back way, up and over Abbey Ridge, because the river's too high to ford. It's a lot farther to go out that way, but we've got no choice. We've seven or eight hours of hard riding ahead of us, so we're going to have to get out of here at daybreak." She tipped her head and listened to the steady downpour on the roof, then shook her head. "Hours of hard riding in the pouring rain. Not a really great ending to your trip, Kev. I'm sorry."

He was sorry, too, although it wasn't the rain that bothered him. He took her in his arms and tried to memorize the feel of holding her, the way her body molded so easily to his, the way she wrapped her arms around his waist and squeezed affectionately.

The top of her head came just below his nose. He tipped her chin and kissed her, forcing a false heartiness into his voice.

"This is the best week I've ever had in my life, but I've heard that all good things come to an end, sooner or later. If we have to go, we have to go. Let's start getting packed."

He'd never felt more dejected in his life.

They left before daybreak the next morning in pouring rain and cold wind. Kevin stopped and looked back at the cabin once when they were high on the mountain, desperate to forge the scene into his memory, but too soon it had disappeared into the mists below as if it had never really been there at all.

From that miserable start, the day went steadily downhill. The wind picked up and blew freezing rain into their faces, chilling them both. Boney refused to climb the long shale draw leading to the top of Abbey Ridge, so Kevin dismounted and had to half haul the stubborn pack animal up the steep bank, adding a solid hour to their ride back to base camp.

At midmorning, the thermos flask containing their hot coffee slipped from Emily's hands and tumbled down a rockslide, never to be seen again.

The most frightening occurrence happened when they stopped for lunch. Sheltering from the driving rain as best they could under a huge tree, they'd just unwrapped their sandwiches when a grizzly ambled out of the bush mere yards away from them.

Emily had been trying to start a fire so they could have a hot drink, and her rifle wasn't within reach. Kevin dived for it, but the shot he fired went over the animal's head.

"Run!" Emily screamed, and Kevin took her advice. They scattered while behind them the horses went wild. The animals were loosely tethered to trees so they could graze, and all three of them broke their lines and stampeded off into the bush.

Kevin made certain he was between Emily and the bear before he stopped and turned, ready to aim and fire at once if necessary.

But the grizzly was obviously intent on some plan of his own. He waddled off into the bush without paying much attention to the frightened humans behind him, stopping only long enough to gulp down their sandwiches, wax paper and all.

Both of them were shaken to the core, and it took them another full hour to round up the skittish horses. But finally, hungry and wetter than ever, they set out once again.

Late that night, bone weary, soaked to the skin and famished, they finally saw the lights of base camp appear like friendly beacons through the darkness and rain.

DESPITE THE HOUR, Laura had hot chili and fresh buns waiting for them, and a steaming pot of coffee. Gertrude and Laura were the only ones still up. The rest of the camp had gone to bed long before. Knowing how wet and cold the ride down would be, they'd thoughtfully heated a tub of water for the makeshift shower just off the kitchen, and Emily and Kevin took turns standing under the spray and scrubbing off the grime from the unpleasant ride.

"Great chili, Laura." Emily's fingers stumbled clumsily over every word. She'd told the other women about the trip out and the grizzly scare, but she hadn't mentioned the week she and Kevin had spent alone together. She couldn't talk about it casually, at least, not yet.

"If chili is so great, then why you don't eat more? Both of you peck at food like birds. What's wrong? Grizzly scare your appetite away?"

Emily assured her sister that the food was wonderful, but there was no denying the fact that she couldn't eat much.

Oddly enough, Kevin wasn't doing much better: His bowl of chili was still half-full, and he was staring down at it as if he'd never seen chili before.

Gertrude, too, seemed distracted; she'd said very little since their arrival, and she hadn't asked questions the way she usually did about a trip.

"I'm beat. That ride down was a killer," Emily tried to explain to Laura. It was true, but it wasn't the trip that bothered her most. She felt not only exhausted, but also morbidly depressed. It was almost impossible to carry on this conversation with her mother and sister—all she could think about was that her time with Kevin was over, and it left her empty inside.

Every step of the miserable way back today, it had become more and more evident to her that her feelings for Kevin were complex and intense. How had she ever thought she could turn them off when they left Grizzly Camp? She'd been painfully aware all day of how it was going to feel to have him leave for good in a day or two.

It was sometime during the endless afternoon—when she was soaked to the skin and shivering, when she thought they'd never get to base camp, and despite the rain and wind and misery, she didn't care—that she'd admitted to herself that she'd fallen hopelessly in love with Kevin Richardson.

The question was, what was she going to do about it?

Several times, she'd considered blurting the truth out to Kevin as they rode stolidly through the mud and the rain, but she'd never summoned up the courage to do so.

Besides, the closer they got to camp, the more he seemed to revert to his old, silent self. Her few attempts at conversation had been met with monosyllabic responses, and she'd finally lapsed into silence, too.

"If you'll excuse me, I think I'll go to bed." Kevin got up all of a sudden and signed a thank-you to Laura, said good-night to them all, gave Emily a long, desperate look, and then hurried out of the cookshack.

Emily felt hot color rise to her hairline. That look had said it all—how much he wanted to hold her, how sorry he was they were back with other people.

Laura, adept at interpreting facial expressions, saw and understood the silent exchange. She caught Emily's eye and winked at her. "We have much to talk about, big sister," she signed with an arch look at Emily.

Gertrude didn't seem to be aware of any undercurrents, however. She sat staring into the dark corners of the room, and soon after Kevin was gone, she sighed and turned to Emily. Her face was somber, and there were worry lines etched into her forehead that hadn't been there before.

"I know I shouldn't dump this on you when you're dead tired, Em, but I'm afraid we won't get a chance to talk in private tomorrow." She spoke and signed in unison, so Laura would be part of the conversation. "The thing is, something very strange has happened and it's worrying me. You remember I sent the check to renew the lease on our guiding territory just before you went up to Grizzly Camp?"

The unusual concern in her mother's voice drove all thoughts of Kevin out of Emily's mind for a moment. "Sure, Mom, I remember. What about it?"

Gertrude frowned and shook her head. "Well, something very strange has happened. It seems that somebody called Pace Developments has taken over our lease. One of the swampers I hired brought the mail in for me yesterday, and my check was returned. There was a formal notice stating that the lease was assumed by this Pace Developments. I tried to phone Victoria and find out what was going on, but it was already late in the day and the offices were closed. By this morning, the radio telephone wasn't working because of the storm, so I still don't know what's going on."

"Why you think these Pace people want our territory?" Laura asked. "Maybe big misunderstanding?" she added, looking at Emily with hope in her blue eyes.

Laura and Gertrude were both silent, watching Emily's reaction, waiting, waiting . . . for what? Emily wondered desperately.

What on earth could this be about? What could she say to them to reassure them? Her mother's words had made her feel sick.

She stared at her mother and sister, trying desperately to think of a logical and innocent explanation for it all, and came up blank.

"Of course, I don't want the clients to know anything is wrong, so we'll have to be discreet while they're around," Gertrude went on at last, her voice bleak. "I'll try to get the telephone to work first thing in the morning, and I'll call Alvin Bleeker and get him to find out what it's all about." Alvin Bleeker was their lawyer.

"That's really all we can do for now, I suppose," Emily said slowly. She got up and went over to her mother, wrapping her arms around her in a fierce bear hug. "Ma, try not to worry. You look tired. It's really late, it was so good of you guys to wait up for us. I'm sure there's a perfectly reasonable explanation for this mess." She wasn't sure at all, but she couldn't think of anything else to say to reassure her mother.

Laura joined them, and the three women embraced for a long moment, seeking mutual comfort. Then Laura yawned and signed, "Wow, I'm tired. Let's all go to bed now, talk again tomorrow. Like you always say, Ma, things look better in the morning."

Gertrude and Laura were both sleeping in the cook-shack, so Emily took a flashlight and headed out alone to her cabin. The disturbing news her mother had told her mingled with the confused feelings she'd been experiencing all day, and suddenly she knew she had to talk to Kevin.

For the past week she'd been with him constantly, sharing every thought and feeling, and now she needed him. Despite her mother's warning about not letting the clients know anything was wrong, she wanted to confide in Kevin. She had to talk to somebody, try to find a logical thread through all of this. She felt threatened and frightened as well as tired, and she needed reassurance. She also knew she had to tell him how she felt about him. Letting him leave without being honest about her feelings wasn't fair to either of them.

She detoured to his cabin. It was in darkness, and she turned off her flash and crept up the steps.

Should she wake him if he was sleeping? She paused outside the door, and finally, as quietly as possible, she lifted the latch and slid inside.

It was like being in a cave. There was no light at all, but she could smell him—smell the clean, male fragrance that was Kevin.

"Emily?" There was hope and profound relief in the whispered question, and she moved in the darkness toward him. "Damn it all, Em, I was praying you'd come.

I know we agreed to be casual and cool once we were down here but, God, I don't think I can pull it off."

"Me, neither."

He was on his feet, and his arms were around her. For long moments, she let him hold her, but when he moved them toward the bed, she shook her head and resisted.

"I can't sleep with you here, Kev, you know that. I just need to talk to you. Something's come up that has Ma really upset. The truth is, it worries me, too. It's the craziest thing, it's about the lease on our territory. It's preposterous, but it sounds like some company's bought out our lease."

She felt him go absolutely still, and a strange fear shot through her. His arms were still around her, and she could feel his heart beating.

"Kevin? Kev, what is it? What's wrong?"

The rhythm of his heartbeat had increased, and his arms tightened on her ribs, until they almost felt like steel bands, trapping her.

"Kev? Tell me what . . ."

She tried to move away from him a bit, and for a moment he resisted, but then he suddenly let her go, and she staggered a little. She heard the bedsprings creak as he sat down hard on the bed.

"Emily." His voice sounded as if it pained him to say her name, and she caught her breath, really afraid now, but still not knowing what it was she feared. She felt for and found the back of the chair, but she couldn't bring herself to sit down. Instead, she gripped it as hard as she could and waited for what seemed an eternity.

"I have to tell you something, but before I do, I want you to know..." He paused and drew in a long, shuddering breath. "God, Em, I didn't think it would turn out this way between us, is what I'm trying to say. I should have talked to you before, but when I came here, I never dreamed..." He paused again, and anger began to replace the dreadful coldness that was making her shiver.

"Kevin, I think you should just tell me whatever it is. Don't beat around the bush this way. I can't handle it. Does it—?" She thought of the way he'd reacted a moment before, and an unthinkable idea struck her.

"My God. It has to do with our lease, doesn't it, Kevin?" She was quite proud of herself for sounding cool, even though her body was trembling so badly she had to clutch the chairback hard to stay upright. She was glad that it was dark, so that he couldn't see the naked fear and devastation she knew was on her face, so that he couldn't see how she was shaking.

"Yeah." There was resignation in his voice now. "Yeah, it does. I knew I should have told you sooner, but I couldn't. The truth is, Emily, Pace Developments is my company, mine and my father's. He's bought up the lease because he wants to put a recreational resort up here."

It took all she had to control her voice. "A resort? Here in the valley? Here in my... in our... guiding territory?"

She imagined he was nodding. "Yeah. I'm afraid so. A big resort, a golf course, swimming pools, riding trails, that sort of thing. Emily, you've got to accept that this valley is ripe for development, that change is inevitable here. You can't stop progress."

The enormity of what he was saying filtered slowly into her consciousness. She felt light-headed, as if she might be going to faint. She fought against it, trying to draw a deep breath and failing. "So...so what were you doing up here, Kevin? Pretending to be a client when you knew all along...?" Her brain felt sluggish, but the answer was there. It was easy, once she knew the facts. "You were scouting out our territory, making sure it was suitable, right?"

"Something like that."

"You were spying on us. And then I ... you ... you made love to me, into the bargain." She sounded quite calm, as if it was a puzzle she'd finally managed to work out. "Well, I guess it helped pass the time, huh, Kevin? Like you said once, there isn't a whole lot to do in this valley, anyway."

"Emily, listen to me, please. What there was between us had nothing to do with this other. This past week has been ... Even though I knew this was going to happen, I couldn't bring myself to spoil what we had together."

"What we had together was obviously a lie. Were you ever going to tell me, or were you just going to hop on a plane and let me find out later?"

"I planned to tell you in the morning. You first, and then Gertrude and Laura."

"God, that's so honorable of you, Kevin." Her voice dripped with sarcasm now, but her throat had a lump in it, and she knew she couldn't hold back the tears too much longer.

"I'll have a talk with your mother and Laura in the morning. But please, Em, let's discuss this rationally, let's try to separate the way we feel for each other from—"

"Rationally? You expect me to be rational about this?" She laughed—a harsh sound more like a sob. "You tell me you plan to wreck my valley, and you want me to be rational?"

She knew he was getting up, coming toward her, and she couldn't bear it. "Emily, if you'll just let me hold you, let me talk to you about this—"

"Don't touch me, please. Get away from me."

She turned and felt blindly for the door, opening it and making her way down the dark steps. To her surprise, she was still holding the flashlight. She flicked it on and ran into the rain.

HE WENT AFTER HER, but she was inside her cabin before he caught up with her. She slammed the door, and he knew she'd locked it.

"Emily, let me in or so help me, I'll smash this door down!" He knew he was yelling. He saw a dim light go on in one of the adjoining cabins. In another moment the other clients would be out here, wondering what the hell was going on. "Open up, Em."

Kevin didn't give a damn about them. It didn't even cross his mind that he wore only his undershorts and a T-shirt, that his feet were bare, that it was three in the morning and pouring rain.

"Emily, do you hear me? I need to talk to you, God-damn it! Now, open this bloody door!"

The door flew open, smashing back against the wall, and the barrel of a rifle poked him in the chest.

"Get away from here, Richardson, or so help me, God, I'll put a bullet right through you."

Her tone was lethal. He knew she actually meant it, and even then he waited a long, tense moment before he moved back a step.

"There's not a single thing you can say to me, you traitor. Your actions said it all. Just leave me alone. Do you understand? Leave—me—alone." She went back inside and slammed the door again, and after a while he became aware that his feet were bare and that it was muddy and cold and extremely wet.

There was nothing to do except go back to his own cabin and wait for morning. Just as she'd said, there really weren't any words that could explain anything.

It was close to dawn before he understood fully what he'd done. He must be a little slack in the head, he thought, not to have realized it sooner.

For the first time in his life, he'd fallen in love with a woman.

And in standard Richardson fashion, he'd ruined it before it had a chance to develop.

10

DAMN, IT WOULDN'T HURT so much if she didn't love him.

Leaning against the cabin door she'd just slammed, her gun cradled in her arms, the hot tears Emily had been holding back trickled slowly down her face.

She'd let herself fall in love with him, and now it seemed he'd taken everything that meant anything to her—her freedom, her happiness, her trust, her valley... God, her valley—and destroyed them one after the other.

Kevin Richardson had known exactly what he was doing. She'd bared her soul to him during the past week, allowing him to see how much she wanted and needed him, showing him in every way how much her job and her valley meant to her. So he knew her as well as anyone ever had—he must have known exactly what the effect would be on her when she learned the truth about him.

And he hadn't given it a second thought.

When the tears finally eased her first agony a little, she thought of Gertrude and Laura, of how they would feel when they understood the magnitude of what had happened to all of them, and she felt ashamed. In their eyes, and in her own, as well, she'd truly been sleeping with the enemy.

The magnitude of the disaster made her feel ill. Elk Valley Adventures was their life, just as it was hers. It was the way they made their living, all of them.

What would become of them now?

She couldn't stop shivering. She wrapped her sleeping bag around herself and lay down on the bed, knowing she wouldn't sleep. As she waited for morning, one thing became clear.

She didn't want Gertrude and Laura to know just yet what Kevin's role in the takeover had been. She couldn't bear having them look at her and witness the extent of her shame and devastation—because they would guess she'd fallen in love with Kevin. They were close, the three of them, and of course Gertrude and Laura would know she was in love with him. Laura knew already, and Gertrude would have seen it last night if she hadn't been so worried about the lease.

He had to leave while she still had some modicum of control, and she was going to have to drive him out to the airport. Gertrude had her own clients to deal with, and Emily didn't want to answer the questions that Gertrude would ask if she suddenly declared she wouldn't deal with him anymore.

It would be agony, having to sit next to him for the hours it would take to get him out, but she'd have to endure it. It would be worth it, she told herself fiercely, just to be rid of him.

The traitor, the Judas, the liar, the cheat.

The man she'd given herself to, body and soul.

Oh, God, she *had* to get rid of him. First thing in the morning.

She waited until dawn, and then watched till he came out of his cabin. She walked over to him through the teeming rainstorm, and she forced her chin high as she stopped a few feet from him.

His shoulders slumped dejectedly, and she refused to acknowledge the pain in his eyes.

"Hello, Em," he said.

"You've got to leave—right away." Her voice was as hard and remote as she could make it, her face a stern mask.

He looked as destroyed as she felt, but she couldn't let herself see that. The rain soaked their hair and dripped off their noses as they stood facing each other like adversaries in some invisible ring.

It was impossible to believe that only the day before, they'd been lovers.

He nodded, accepting her decision. "I'd planned to go right away, anyhow. My things are packed. I want to explain everything to your mother and Laura first, though, Emily."

"I don't want you to explain to them. I—" Her voice came near to breaking and she controlled it with an effort. "I want to tell them myself, when I'm ready. They still think there's been a mistake about the lease, and I'd rather they went on thinking that, for now. There's the other clients to consider—Ma and Laura won't be at their best if they find out what's really happening. I don't want Laura upset right now because of the baby. It's easier this way."

He studied her, the lines in his face deeply etched and rigid. There was something formidable about him this morning. "Please," she forced herself to say.

Finally, he nodded. "I don't like doing it that way, but if that's what you want, okay. When do you want to head out?"

"As soon as you're ready."

"I'm ready now."

"I'll get my keys."

THE ROAD, NEVER A WORK of art, was unbelievably bad this morning. Rain had been sheeting down steadily for four days now, and in several places small rockslides had all but obliterated the path. The Jeep slid and slithered through mud and bounced over obstacles for the first ten miles, but then at one particularly difficult spot, it slipped sideways into the ditch, tilting over at a precarious angle, wheels spinning fruitlessly as Emily tried to get them back on the trail.

Till now, she'd been almost grateful for the terrible conditions because they forced her to concentrate all her attention on driving. Several times, Kevin had tried to talk to her, but she'd pretended she was as deaf as Laura. He'd finally given up and they rode in silence.

When she got out and sank up to her ankles in mud, however, she knew she was going to have to enlist Kevin's help—she couldn't dig them out and drive at the same time.

She steeled herself to speak to him, but before she could say anything, he was already beside her, getting the shovel out of the toolbox. She reached out to snatch it from him.

"I'll dig, you drive," she ordered curtly.

He hung on to the handle and shook his head. "Forget it, Emily. You drive, I'll dig."

She looked at him, chin jutted out stubbornly, but there was an implacable expression on his face that convinced her. She got into the Jeep and slammed the door viciously. When he shouted at her to hit the gas, she did so with a vengeance. She knew mud was spraying all over him, and she smiled grimly.

Take that, Pace Developments.

It took them the better part of an hour to get the Jeep back on what masqueraded as a road, and by the time they had, Kevin was unrecognizable. Mud had spattered his clothing and his face, and his hands were filthy. He didn't say anything, but his expression was grim.

"You're a mess. Well, I guess your company's going to have to spend a small fortune to upgrade this road, Mr. Richardson," Emily said sweetly. "We couldn't afford to have it done, but of course money's no object to big operators like you and your father, right? We're real small-fry to corporations like Pace. You probably even believe you're doing us backwoods bumpkins a favor by coming in here and showing us how to run a resort, isn't that right?"

She wanted to make him furious. She wanted to fight with him, really fight. She wanted to scream out all the things that were hurting her so much she thought she'd die of them.

He gave her a warning look, but baiting him didn't work.

"I've said I feel terrible about this, Emily." His voice was low and in control. "There's not a whole lot more I can say about it. I'd stop the development if I could, but I'm not in this alone. There are investors to be considered, contractors. It's company business."

"Right. Of course. Business is business, I ought to know that. Where you come from, people don't matter, right?" She stepped viciously on the gas, recklessly ignoring the fact that the roadway ahead was downright dangerous. He gripped the armrest and his head collided with the roof as she hit a pothole deep enough to bury the Jeep in.

"Look out, Em—"

Kevin's shout came an instant after she saw the empty space gaping where the bridge was supposed to be. She stood on the brakes, and the Jeep careered from one side to the other and finally came to rest inches from the edge of the riverbank. There was a steep drop straight down a muddy slope with boulders at the bottom.

The motor died, and there was only the sound of the incessant rain, drumming on the roof.

"The damned bridge must've washed out," she said stupidly. She was trembling, imagining what might have happened if she hadn't been able to stop in time. They might both be unconscious, or dead, down there in the mud.

Then slowly the consequences of the washout dawned on her and she slumped over the wheel, wondering what the hell she'd ever done to deserve this. There was no way out now, no way to get to the airstrip or even to town. She was stuck with Kevin Richardson until the bridge was fixed.

There was silence for a long, dismal time. "Well," she finally said, "I guess there's no choice. You'll just have to come back to camp and wait out the storm."

Her life was taking on all the elements of a nightmare, with a few bad jokes thrown in for good measure.

THE NEWS OF THE washed-out bridge kept her mother from questioning Emily too closely about why she was taking Kevin out before breakfast.

It didn't work with Laura. After another meal neither Emily nor Kevin touched, Laura beckoned Emily into her little room and closed the door.

"What gives?" she demanded, pulling Emily down on the bed beside her. "You look like stone image, he looks like mugging victim, no one talks. So explain. Now."

"The Jeep got stuck. He got covered with mud. We had a fight."

"Over what?" Laura absentmindedly rubbed her burgeoning tummy. She'd gotten noticeably larger in the past week, Emily thought distractedly. She could actually see the baby moving under the long T-shirt her sister wore. She reached out a hand and placed it tenderly on Laura's abdomen, fascinated by the movement of her niece or nephew.

"This baby's getting big. You aren't worried about going into labor up here, are you, Laura?"

Laura wasn't the least bit distracted. "Nope, no chance. You fight with Kevin over what?"

Emily shook her head in exasperation, wishing to God Laura would leave her alone. But Laura wouldn't give up until she had a satisfactory answer—Emily knew that from past experience.

"Fought over everything" was all she could think of to sign.

"That means over nothing. But you love him?" It was a statement of fact more than a question.

Emily gritted her teeth and looked away, not at all sure how long her shaky composure would last.

Laura touched her cheek gently to get her attention. "Kevin loves you, too. I can tell by how he looks at you."

Rage smoldered in Emily. If her sister only knew exactly how ridiculous it was to even imagine Kevin loved her.

Well, Laura would know soon enough. It wasn't a secret that could be kept long. Gertrude's radio phone was totally out of commission this morning, so she hadn't been able to call the lawyer, and with the bridge out, no mail would be coming in, either.

It bought Emily some time, and for that small favor she was grateful.

Laura was watching her and frowning. "I think it hard for Parker women to love," she said thoughtfully. Patting her belly, she added, "Physical love we can do fine, but—" she put a hand on her heart and then touched her forehead "—here, and here, it's hard for us." Her pixie face was somber, her blue eyes troubled. "Maybe too independent, all of us," she added. "Right?"

Emily tried to smile and failed. "Right," she lied.

Her problem was, she hadn't stayed independent enough.

IT RAINED DAY AND NIGHT—not just a gentle misting, but an all-out downpour accompanied by high winds and several dramatic thunder-and-lightning displays. There was nothing to do but wait it out, and soon everyone's nerves were on edge.

Emily couldn't sleep, and time seemed endless, trapped in her tiny cabin during the long nights. The days were worse. Having to be around Kevin was torture, and even though he disappeared for hours each day, apparently walking or jogging in the pouring rain, it was impossible to avoid him for long. There was nowhere for any of them to be except alone in their cabins or with the others in the larger building.

Misery made her outrageously bad-tempered, and even flirtatious Frank Livetti soon began staying out of her way as much as possible after she snapped his head off a couple of times.

Frank and Sam and Melvin passed the time playing endless games of gin rummy, but it was obvious they were on edge.

The strained atmosphere was part of it, but it also seemed as if the men had only now realized exactly how pregnant Laura was. It had also dawned on them that they were trapped with her, and they were all decidedly uncomfortable about it.

If she so much as sneezed, they exchanged uneasy looks and became restless. A gas pain could cause quiet hysteria. She had a cramp in her leg that created major panic. They fell over themselves trying to keep Laura from lifting anything, and as a result were constantly underfoot and in the way.

On the afternoon of the fourth day, Emily actually overheard Sam Lucas assigning Melvin and Frank tasks if anything should happen with Laura.

It would have struck her as funny any other time, but now it simply added to Emily's irritation, and she exploded at all of them.

"Instead of sitting around here like useless clods, why don't you men get out and chop some wood or something? You're pathetic, the whole works of you, sitting around here doing nothing." She leveled a lethal glare at all of them, and within moments they were struggling into rain gear and there was all but a stampede to get outside.

Gertrude was stirring a pot of stew. She'd heard the whole thing and she gave Emily a considering look.

"In case you've forgotten, Em, those men are our clients. They're paying guests, and it's up to us to make this as pleasant for them as possible. I shouldn't have to even remind you of that. Chasing them out in the pouring rain to chop wood isn't going to make them want to come back next year, and we rely on return business."

"I don't care if I never see any of them again," Emily muttered. And she wouldn't, anyway. Thanks to Kevin, there wasn't any "next year" for Elk Valley Adventures. She felt like giving in to the hysterics that had been just under the surface for days now.

What would become of her and Laura and Gertrude? To stop herself from screaming, Emily began taking everything down from the shelves, banging cans and baking dishes onto the counter with a vengeance, and slopping disinfectant into a bowl to scrub with.

"Laura just cleaned those shelves." Gertrude sounded exasperated. "What the hell is biting you, Em? If it's this lease thing, well, I'm worried sick about it, too, but there's nothing we can find out with the bridge gone and the radio not working. The least we can do is be professional and not allow it to affect the clients."

It was on the tip of Emily's tongue to spill out the whole sorry business. But she choked it back and set about scrubbing down everything she could reach.

Although she tried to pretend otherwise, the tension was getting to Gertrude, as well. She almost snapped Sam's head off at suppertime when he tried to make a joke about being marooned with her like the people had been on *Gilligan's Island*.

The only person unaffected by it all was Laura. Calm and serene, she cooked and baked delicious treats for them all, and flashed her sunny smile often. Emily found her sister's good nature endlessly irritating.

Finally, on the fifth morning, just when Emily was considering mass murder and then suicide, the rain stopped and faint sunlight appeared. Everyone flooded outside and stayed there all morning.

Just before noon, Emily was outside forking hay to the horses when she glanced up and saw a bedraggled and soaking-wet Jackson Briggs loping down the road toward camp.

Puffing his way over to her, the big, bearded logger didn't even bother saying hello. His brown eyes were frantic as he panted out, "How's Laura? God, she hasn't gone into labor or anything, has she? I've been going berserk, worrying about her and the baby. Where is she?"

Emily hastily assured him that her sister was fine. "I saw her fifteen minutes ago—she was baking bread. She's fat, but she's wonderfully healthy, Jackson. In fact, she looks a lot better than you do right now. You shouldn't run like that, you're going to heart-attack. And where did you run from, anyhow? How did you get across the river?"

"I swam. I've been going right nuts. I only found out yesterday the bridge was out, so I brought guys from my crew up to rebuild it. But I couldn't wait, so I swam across."

Emily thought of the freezing water and the ferocious current, and her admiration for Jackson went up several notches.

"C'mon in and get some dry things on. You can borrow clothes from Sam, he won't mind. And then you can have some lunch."

Lunch was decidedly strained. Laura's good nature evaporated with Jackson's arrival. She made it plain she was furious with him for being foolhardy enough to ford the river when it was in flood, and she reminded him in no uncertain terms that she was capable of taking care of herself. They had a fight about it and she burned the bread, which made her even angrier. Jackson made the mistake of insisting she come straight out with him as soon as the bridge was fixed, and she made an exceptionally rude sign that everyone, unfortunately, understood.

Emily made a point of sitting as far away from Kevin as she could get, and he'd stopped addressing any remarks to her, because she ignored anything he said.

Jackson looked about ready to explode, and Laura had finally locked herself in her room, slamming the door and refusing to come out.

Strained silence reigned at the table. Finally Jackson sighed and shrugged philosophically. "Any of you guys want to come down and give us a hand with the bridge? We could sure use some help, and working from both sides, we'd get it done quicker," he announced. The men all leaped at the chance.

"Take the truck," Gertrude suggested.

After the men drove off down the road, she turned to her daughters. "I'm ashamed of both of you," Gertrude exploded. "At least Laura has the lame excuse that pregnancy may be affecting her brain, but *you*, Emily—I'm disgusted with the way you're treating Kevin. There's no excuse for it. You're being childish. If you had some lovers' quarrel, surely you could reconcile it enough to be civil to the man. I quite like him. He's a gentleman."

Emily knew the time had finally come to tell Gertrude and Laura the horrifying facts about Pace Developments and Kevin Richardson. It was a burden she couldn't bear alone any longer.

"Pace Developments, the company that bought out our lease, is owned by Kevin and his father."

And then it was like a nightmare, watching Gertrude and Laura absorb all the ramifications of what she was saying. They were shocked and horrified, and neither of them could accept at first the full extent of Kevin's deceit.

Telling them was like going through it all over again herself. As she'd known it would be, the hardest thing for Emily was their full understanding of how she felt about Kevin, and then their compassion for her in his utter betrayal of her.

Typically, Gertrude became furious before long. If Kevin had been nearby, Emily was sure her mother would have attacked him physically.

"What can we do to stop them?" It was Laura who asked the practical question finally, and the three of them spent energy and time trying desperately to figure out a way, but they each soon realized it was impossible.

It was Gertrude who summed it up for all of them. "We haven't the money or the political influence necessary for a full-scale fight. We're beaten, girls. There's nothing left to do but accept defeat."

For the first time she could ever remember, Emily thought her mother looked old.

THE MEN CAME BACK LATE that evening. The bridge was in place, and the hard physical effort had been cathartic after the dismal days of inactivity.

As he always did, Kevin looked first for Emily, but she wasn't around. Then he noticed the drawn, angry faces that Gertrude and Laura turned on him and knew that Emily had told them.

It was a relief; he'd felt like a traitor, and it was much better to have it all out in the open.

"Jackson's offered me a ride back to town tonight, so I'll leave now," he said quietly. "I'd like to say goodbye to Emily. Do you know where she is?"

Gertrude had her arms folded over her chest, and the look she gave him was chilling. "She's gone to check one of the other camps—she won't be back tonight. I think leaving is a very good idea. Emily's told us about your company's takeover of our land."

"Yes, I thought she had. I wanted to tell you myself, but Emily asked me not to."

"Coming here was a rotten, dirty thing to do, Kevin Richardson." Her voice was low and filled with contempt.

He met her venomous gaze with a long, steady look. "It was, Gertrude, and I'm deeply sorry for the way I've hurt you. But I'll never be sorry I came," he insisted, looking her straight in the eye. "In many ways, these past weeks have been the best of my life."

"Just get out of my sight," Gertrude spat at him, then turned her back and walked away.

He went over to Laura, and the look of betrayal and hurt in her clear blue eyes was almost his undoing. "I thought you were friend," she signed accusingly.

"True" was all he could manage. He reached out and touched her cheek gently. "Thank you for all the good meals and for helping me learn to sign. I'll never forget you. Take care of your big sister for me, okay?"

She stared at him, accusingly. "You hurt my sister worst of all. What you will do about it?"

The question was both simple and profound. For a moment, words and signs both failed him. What in hell was there to do? How could he ever make it up to Emily? He struggled for an answer, and then signed the simple truth.

"I don't know yet. I'll think of something. I promise you I'll think of some way, because I love her."

The sign for love was crossed hands, folded on his chest and drawn in close to his heart. It was a graphic, powerful sign, one he'd never made before.

But he could tell Laura didn't believe him, and he didn't blame her for it.

THE RIDE BACK TO TOWN with Jackson was long and tedious. His crew was riding in the back of the van he was driving, but they fell asleep soon after leaving base camp. Kevin sat next to Jackson in the front seat, and the two men exchanged comments on the weather, the political situation in B.C. and the players in the NFL.

"You married?" Jackson asked next.

"Divorced, long ago," Kevin told him.

"You get to know Laura much, being up at camp and all?" There was wistfulness in the logger's tone, and Kevin felt empathy for him.

"She and Emily taught me some sign language. I used to understand it but I'd forgotten a lot. Yeah, I got to know her. She's a fine woman."

Jackson nodded morosely. "She is that, but she's as ornery as a mule. That's my baby she's carrying, y'know, and I want more than anything to marry her, but she won't. She believes that if the baby is deaf, it'd cause problems." He squinted out into the darkness and swore. "How the hell she figures that is beyond me. She's deaf and I love her so damned much I'd like to strangle her at times and, goddamn it, I'm a peaceable man."

To anyone else, that might seem a contradiction in terms, but Kevin understood perfectly how the Parker women could drive a man to mayhem.

"I feel the same about Emily. Although she's got good reason to hate me, no doubt about it." Kevin heard himself telling Jackson about Pace Developments and the lease takeover.

When he was finished, Jackson whistled.

"Emily'll be some upset about that. I've known her since high school. She loves this valley more than anybody I ever met. One of my buddies was sweet on Emily at one time, but he never got to first base with her."

"She's a strong woman. I admire that."

Jackson agreed. "But she's gonna be the one hurting the worst about this development you're talking about, y'know." He negotiated a particularly bad pothole and then turned to look at Kevin.

"If you care about her like you say, it's gonna be tough getting to first base with her after this. She's not gonna see anything except that she's losing Elk Valley Adventures—not for a hell of a long while."

"I'll just have to wait, then."

Jackson grunted. "Join the club."

11

BACK IN VANCOUVER, Kevin phoned his father.

"Where the hell you been?" Barney greeted him, his tone accusing. "You were due back well over a week ago. You got the picture layout for the investors ready? I been doing some fancy footwork at this end—they want action."

Nothing had changed.

Everything had changed.

"Ever try saying, 'Hello, Kevin, how you doing?' Nice talking to you, too, Dad. I'll see you in the office. I'm taking tomorrow off, so it'll be Wednesday, probably about ten. Talk to you then."

Ignoring the surprised spluttering coming out of the receiver, Kevin hung up and unplugged the phone.

He was bone weary, mentally and physically exhausted, and all he could think of was Emily. He had to figure out a plan of action.

KEVIN ARRIVED AT WORK before nine on Wednesday morning.

"Barney's back there in his office—he got in extra early this morning," their middle-aged secretary, Ruth Wilkins, told him with a smile. "Shall I bring you both some coffee?"

"Please, Ruth."

His father was always at work at the crack of dawn— no surprise, considering that Barney's entire life was Pace Developments.

He made his way to his father's office and found him standing behind his desk, studying a file folder crammed with maps. He was a big man, more than a little overweight for the past few years, but handsome. Kevin had inherited his long bones and broad shoulders from his father.

In typical fashion, Barney didn't waste time asking how Kevin's trip had been, or what Elk Valley Adventures really consisted of. Instead he bulldozed right in, as always, bitching a little more about the extra days Kevin had been away and the fact that he hadn't come to work the moment he returned. Then Barney moved straight into the nuts and bolts of the proposed resort.

What would roads cost, had Kevin scouted out good locations for different aspects of the resort, had he managed to get decent pictures that would look good to investors? And Kevin listened and recognized clearly how devoid their relationship was of real communication. He might have been a stranger, a casual employee Barney had hired. For the first time, Kevin allowed it to hurt.

Ruth came in with a tray, and when she was gone, Kevin took a mug and sank down in one of the deep leather armchairs.

"I want to talk to you, Barney."

"What the hell do you think we're doing?" Barney drew on a cigar and blew the smoke out in a stream. There were already ashes on his tie. "Now what about the local contractors? Were you able to—?"

"Barney, will you for God's sake shut up and listen to me for a change?" Anger and reckless abandon overwhelmed Kevin. He sprang to his feet, smashed his mug down on the desk in front of him and glared at his father.

Barney stared back at him, astonished, forgetting about his cigar for once. It hung limply from the corner of his mouth.

"Take it easy. What the hell's gotten into you all of a sudden? You run into problems back there?"

"No. Yes. Goddamn it, Barney, I'm fed up with— with the way things are between us, that's what's gotten into me. For once in my life, I want to have a real conversation with you, about something besides business." Kevin shoved his fingers through his hair, trying to dredge up the words he needed, feeling the old inadequacy welling up inside and fighting it with all his might.

"You're my father, for Christ's sake, and I don't remember a single time when you really talked to me about anything that mattered. When *we* talked, father and son."

This was hard. He felt embarrassed, as if what he was trying to do wasn't manly in his father's eyes, but he persevered anyway.

"Talking's never been my strong point, but it sure as hell isn't yours, either, Barney." Some of his anger was dissipating, but he was determined to carry on. He took a deep breath. "I guess we're alike that way—not saying much that really matters to each other. But you know, you're not getting any younger, and neither am I. So let's give this a shot while we still have a chance. Agreed?" He met Barney's stunned gaze with a level look, and waited.

Barney remembered his cigar and closed his mouth around it. "What is this, some of this newfangled male-bonding crap or something?" he snarled. His face grew quite red, but he took a mug of coffee and sat down, careful to keep the desk between him and his son. He eyed Kevin warily, as if he thought he'd taken leave of his senses.

"Calm down here, will ya, Kevin? You're not making sense. What the hell you mean, we never talk? We talk all the time, day in, day out."

"About business. There happens to be more to life than business, Barney."

His father's forehead furrowed and he spluttered, "You're beginning to sound just like—" He stopped abruptly and swore under his breath. Then he looked past Kevin, out the window at the tugboats on the river, his mouth twisted into a grimace.

Kevin's smile was sad. "Were you going to say just like my mother, Barney? She's another one of the things we never talk about. And maybe we should."

Barney looked ready to explode. "What the hell happened to you back there in that valley? You and I never had any trouble before. What's brought all this garbage up all of a sudden?"

Kevin met his father's belligerent gaze.

"This garbage, as you call it, is important to me. There're things about my mother I'd like to know, and there's nobody to ask except you."

The next part was the worst. He'd never in his life admitted weakness to Barney—not since he was five and told his father he was afraid to go off to boarding school.

"Be a man," Barney had ordered then. "What the hell are you, a coward? Goddamn it, men don't snivel or whine over anything."

It was the last time he'd told his father how he really felt about anything—until now. Emily had said he should try, and by God, he was going to do it.

"What happened back in the Elk Valley was . . . I . . . I fell in love, Dad. With a woman named Emily Parker."

Barney took out his cigar and set it carelessly in the overflowing ashtray on the desk.

"Parker. Parker. Isn't that the name of the people—?"

"Who ran Elk Valley Adventures, yeah. The people we've just successfully put out of business. I told her what we were doing, and it hurt her bad. She doesn't want anything to do with me, and that's pretty understandable right now. But the thing is, I love her and I intend to marry her, even if it takes me the next fifty years to wear her down."

Kevin heard himself say it, and realized it was true. Maybe this talking was good, after all. His mouth obviously knew things his brain hadn't gotten around to recognizing yet.

Now came the part that would make Barney froth at the mouth. "First off, I want to know if there's any way we can drop this resort project."

Barney's eyes rolled heavenward. "Holy shit, you've gone plumb crazy. You're thinking with your pecker here instead of your head. Drop it, just because you got the hots for this broad?"

Kevin's eyes narrowed dangerously. "Watch it, Barney. Her name is Emily, and I told you I'm in love with her."

"Sorry. Sorry about that." Barney seemed to look at Kevin and really see him for the first time that morning. "No. We can't pull out now, Kevin. You know the figures better than I do—you know how much we already got invested. And there's the backers, we can't let them down or we'll never get to first base in this town again. Besides, that area is ripe for exactly what we've got planned. If we don't move in now, somebody else will in the near future—and maybe do a hell of a lot worse damage than we plan to."

Barney was right. Reluctantly, Kevin admitted it. Nothing was going to preserve Emily's valley forever—redevelopment was inevitable.

Maybe there was a remote valley in northern Alberta or the North West Territories he could buy for her. He was going to look into it, because he was going to win her back, no matter what it took.

Right now, though, there were things he could do to make her life at least marginally easier. "Then I propose we generously recompense the Parker women financially for the loss of their business and their camps."

Barney eyes bulged out and he started shaking his head, but here Kevin was adamant. "It makes good business sense, Barney. You have to pay them what the buildings are worth anyhow, and if they chose to, they could probably make a pretty good case against us in court for loss of income, so let's offer them a generous settlement up front and avoid a lot of hassle. And I also want to delay the start of the project until next spring, so they can fulfill the contracts they have for this season."

"Absolutely not. It's still early spring—we got the whole summer and fall to really make some headway. We'll lose money...."

It took an hour of tough negotiation, but at last, with reservations, Barney agreed to most of what Kevin wanted.

"You're a stubborn son of a gun when you get your mind made up, I'll say that for you," he told Kevin, and there was just a hint of pride in his voice. "Now that you got what you wanted, you can damn well buy me lunch." Barney took his raincoat from the closet and struggled into it. His voice was muffled when he said,

"Your mother was like that, y'know. Stubborn as all get-out when she wanted something. Before she got sick. Guess you're like her in some ways."

It wasn't much, but it was a beginning.

LAURA WENT INTO LABOR July 17th, near midnight on a Saturday, two full weeks past her due date. She was considerate enough to choose a time when one set of clients had just left and the next hadn't arrived, so Emily was able to be in the delivery room when her nine-pound six-ounce nephew was born.

"Looks just like his father," Laura declared when the wailing, scarlet-faced infant was placed in her arms.

Emily thought he was the most adorable baby ever born, and it was obvious Jackson Briggs thought so, too.

Obstinate to the last moment, Laura had finally allowed Emily to call Jackson only an hour before, and he'd broken all speed limits getting to the hospital to see his son born. The doctor had assured them it was an easy delivery, although Jackson barely survived it.

The husky logger had been in danger of passing out during the final stages of the birth, but the expression on his face now as he stood looking down at Laura and his son left no doubt about how much he loved both of them. There was adoration in his eyes, along with a suspicion of tears.

"Has his mother's stubborn chin," he signed clumsily. He'd been taking signing lessons for the past month, and it was becoming more and more evident that he was gradually overcoming Laura's objections.

Emily watched them, tears pouring down her cheeks, delighted for her sister, but feeling as if her heart was tearing in two.

Most of the time, she didn't allow herself to consciously think about Kevin, although she couldn't stop the pain—an aching agony that nothing eased, day or night. She did her best to ignore it, but she couldn't sleep more than an hour or so at a time, and her usually voracious appetite had all but disappeared. Her jeans were starting to hang dangerously low on what had been her hips.

She wanted to hate him for what he'd done but she couldn't even accomplish that.

And tonight, filled with the miracle of watching this baby born, against all reason she longed for him and what would never be. She wanted to be with Kevin, she wanted to someday hold his baby in her arms as Laura now held Jackson's—because nothing changed the fact that she loved him.

She cursed herself for being weak, for being a traitor to her family and to herself, but reason didn't work on her heart.

When she got her period, reassuring her that all was well, that no child would result from their lovemaking at Grizzly Camp, she'd spent an entire night sobbing her heart out, appreciating as never before the decisions Laura had made during the past nine months.

Laura had never once for a moment considered abortion.

Emily knew if she'd been pregnant, she'd have kept Kevin's baby, too. Against all reason.

Gertrude raced in just in time to hold her grandson before the nurse bustled him off to the nursery. Sam Lucas was with her. Sam seemed to have booked for the entire damn summer with Elk Valley Adventures. Emily hated to think what was happening to his veterinary practice while he chased around the valley with Gertrude. Didn't animals in San Diego have health problems during July and August, for God's sake?

"I tried to call you a couple of times but you were out," Emily told her just a little accusingly. Her mother was spending a lot of time with Sam these days, and Emily wasn't sure she liked it.

"Sam and I had to drive up the pass for hay, and then we went out to dinner. Laura was feeling just fine when we left."

Gertrude sounded defensive, and Emily suddenly felt ashamed. Her mother seemed to have taken out a new lease on life in the past weeks. After the initial shock had worn off, Gertrude accepted the loss of their business in a way that startled Emily. Pace had offered them an enormous financial settlement, and the relief from continual monetary worries seemed to have done Gertrude a world of good. She'd started having her hair done, had even bought some new clothes. In fact, she was wearing a new dress tonight, a pretty blue cotton that emphasized her slender figure.

It was mean-spirited of her to make her mother feel guilty, Emily admitted. She put an arm around Gertrude's shoulders and gave her a hug. "Isn't that baby of ours absolutely gorgeous?"

"Looks just like his grandma," Sam commented with a soulful look at Gertrude, and Emily privately thought he resembled a lovesick sheep.

But Gertrude smiled at him and actually let him hold her hand as they left the hospital together, and Emily felt more alone and lonely than ever as she followed them out. She waved cheerfully enough as they drove away, and then climbed into Matilda for the long drive home.

THE BURNING QUESTION was, what was she going to do with her life? The problem plagued her all that long summer as she guided and cooked and pretended to smile at the last clients Elk Valley Adventures would ever have.

The day arrived in late September when she drove the final group of them to the airport and then headed home, feeling bereft.

She pulled into the yard, smiling at the sight of the baby carriage on the wide veranda, with Caleb crouched protectively beneath it.

Caleb had taken it upon himself to protect little Alexander Robert Jackson Parker-Briggs with his life. He took his responsibility seriously. He stood and growled ominously, showing his teeth, when Emily walked over to the carriage.

"Caleb, you're a nut case. I'm the kid's aunt, for gosh sakes. Now lie down and shut up."

Caleb settled a bit sheepishly as Emily picked the baby out of the carriage and walked over to the old, scarred rocking chair, settling the warm, fragrant bundle in her arms with familiar ease.

She could hear Laura banging pots around inside the house, probably making a chocolate cake for Jackson. It seemed she was always making cakes for Jackson these days, although she continued to refuse to marry him. Instead, she'd decided to move in with him.

"See how we make out as family first, then make decisions later," she said.

So Laura and Alex were moving into Jackson's place next weekend, and Emily was stealing every opportunity to spoil Alex rotten before that happened.

"Well, big fellow, you catch any fish or shoot any bears while I was gone this morning?"

Alex looked up at her and smiled one of his wide, goofy, baby grins, melting her heart. He loved being talked to. He cried at loud noises, which made his grandma and aunt ecstatic, because it proved he could hear. His mother and father were less affected by his hearing or lack of it; they'd discussed all the issues that either eventuality would present and apparently dealt with them satisfactorily between themselves.

"So your mum and dad are taking you to live with them, which I figure is grossly unfair, and your grandma is flying off to San Diego for a couple weeks with old Sam for some kind of wild holiday. There's no accounting for taste, huh? Honestly, kid, you got yourself a set of nutty relatives, for sure. Except for me, of course."

It bothered her that losing Elk Valley Adventures hadn't seemed to affect Gertrude and Laura the way it had her. They'd brushed themselves off and gotten on with their lives.

"It'll be a good thing, actually, if your grandma decides to hook up with Sam Lucas, Alex. Knowing her, she'll probably never agree to marry him, but so what? They'll be fun to introduce to your friends someday—two old people living in sin."

Alex cooed and found his thumb to suck.

"They asked me to go with them to California, y'know. Talk about three wheels on a wagon. Mind you, I was touched by the invitation, but of course, I turned it down. What the dickens would I do in California?"

For that matter, what on earth was she going to do *here*?

"So that leaves your old Auntie Em all on her own, right?"

She'd found she could talk to Alex. He was a great listener, and he didn't mind when tears occasionally dripped off her chin and into his blankets. But she wasn't crying today. She'd made up her mind to stop crying. There really wasn't any point to it. It was a sinful waste of energy and time.

She'd decided to take control, to use the next couple of weeks while she was alone to do some hard thinking about her life and what she was going to do with it.

She also wanted to say goodbye to her valley in her own way, so she'd decided to pack in to Grizzly Camp and face the ghosts that waited for her there.

Maybe then she could make some decisions, move ahead instead of staying mired in the memories that haunted her.

"Too bad you can't ride, young man, and of course, you're far too dependent on your mama for nourishment. Otherwise, you could come with me. Maybe next year...." But she reminded herself that by the time Alex learned to ride, the Valley would be changed forever.

It wasn't only Pace Developments that was changing the valley, either.

What Kevin had said about other development being inevitable had already proven true; over the summer, wealthy investors had begun building a lavish guest ranch at an isolated lake that hadn't even had an access road until last month. Two new motels were under construction in Elkford, and there was talk of a world-class golf course to be built in a remote meadow where moose had been the only inhabitants until now.

"I'll take a ton of pictures for you, kid, so you can see the Elk Valley the way it used to be," she whispered to Alex. But then the memory of Kevin rose in her mind, and once again, tears moistened Alex's soft yellow blanket.

Damnation. How could she miss someone this much, while at the same time despise him for what he'd done to her?

WHEN SHE RODE DOWN Abbey Ridge three days later and saw the meadow and the cabin, her heart started to hammer.

It all looked just the way it had when they'd left it that rainy morning in May. She unsaddled Cody and put him in the corral, and then she opened the cabin door.

God, it was painful, being here. She kept wanting to look over her shoulder, in case he might be there somewhere behind her in the shadows. She opened the shutters to let the fresh evening air in, and then tossed her gear into one of the bedrooms, being careful to choose the room they hadn't slept in.

Outside, the poplar trees were blazing masses of crimson and orange and gold, signaling that fall was well advanced and winter not far off. There was already snow in the higher reaches of the Rockies. The meadow grass was yellow; it had been a dry summer. But Honeymoon Lake, glimmering turquoise green in the twilight, evoked memories of that first evening here with Kevin, and the way he'd tricked her into jumping into the icy water.

Until now, she'd repressed all memories of him, because remembering was too damn painful. For a long time, she'd tried to hate him—tried with all the passion and fierceness of her nature—but it never quite worked.

She hated what he'd done, but she didn't hate him.

She turned in a slow circle, surveying the towering mountains and the valley she loved. This had been her world, this wilderness. It represented her career, her deepest comfort, her heart's home. She'd been safe and happy here.

Not anymore. It was a barren wilderness without Kevin beside her. It wasn't home anymore.

Could even a city like Vancouver, God forbid, feel like home—if she were with someone she loved?

As the evening deepened, she wandered back and built a fire in the cookstove. She heated up some soup and lit the lantern, and then gradually she allowed herself to recall the good times they'd had.

Kevin. She let his image fill her senses—soft dark hair, deep-set eyes, the creases in his cheeks when he grinned. She'd teased him about having dimples and he'd been scandalized. She recalled his physical strength, his good nature, his quiet humor, the difficulty he'd had talking about his lonely childhood and his confused feelings about his mother. It had taken courage to finally talk about everything, and she admired him for that.

When night fell, she wandered into the bedroom, turned the small lantern off, and in the darkness, crawled into her sleeping bag. This was the time she missed him the most, the time when her body longed for his touch. She remembered what it had felt like, having him touch her here . . . and here. . . .

At last she got up and dragged her sleeping bag and pillow into the other bedroom. She found the exact hollow in the ancient springs where their entwined bodies had fitted, and she curled herself into a ball and pretended he was there beside her.

The coyotes howled for a long time, sounding eerie and forlorn. Gradually she recognized that there was nothing here for her anymore—without Kevin.

She'd stay for a few days, and then she'd ride out.

Maybe she'd try and write him a letter or something.

Sometime before dawn she finally fell asleep.

KEVIN HAD RENTED A CAR at the airport and driven to the valley. He'd phoned Jackson several times over the summer to find out how Emily was, but he hadn't been in contact for a while now.

He knew that her last clients must be gone, however; the season was over. He drove up the valley, admiring the fall foliage and remembering that first trip with Emily.

When he turned into the Parkers' driveway, his heart was thudding against his ribs. Would she be home? Would she be willing to listen to what he had to say? One way or the other, he was going to make her listen.

The pole corral was empty, and even the barn looked deserted. He stopped the car in front of the house, and it took a few minutes to realize that no one was living here right now. Even Caleb was absent.

He got out and walked to the door, knocking several times just in case, but of course, there was no answer.

Fear made his gut contract. It looked as if no one was living here *anymore*. What if Emily had gone away? What if she'd met someone else and married him on the rebound? The thought hadn't crossed his mind before, but suddenly he was obsessed with it.

He walked back to his car and started it. He was halfway up the lane when an old red Thunderbird coupe wheeled into the driveway.

Laura was driving, with her baby in a seat beside her.

Kevin pulled over and got out, and Laura stopped. For a moment they just looked at each other.

"Hello, Laura. Fine big boy you've got there," Kevin signed at last. "Congratulations." Relief spilled through him when she finally smiled and got out of the car.

"Glutton. Eats all the time," she told him, her face ablaze with pride. "Thank you for gifts. Clothes should fit him soon."

Kevin had sent Alex the smallest pair of elaborate cowboy boots he could find, along with miniature Levi's, a Western shirt, and a tiny Stetson.

Jackson had sent a thank-you note, but there'd been no word from Laura.

She looked up at him now, her clear blue gaze as direct and honest as ever. "I wondered if you'd come back," her fingers said.

"I have to see Emily. Where is she? There's no one home."

"Mom is in San Diego. Alex and I move to Jackson's house, couple of miles away. Horses are with neighbor. We took Caleb while Mom's away."

Inside the car, the baby had started to fuss. Unable to hear him, Laura didn't realize it yet, but Kevin knew that when she did, she was likely to get in and drive away.

She still hadn't said where Emily was, and Kevin realized she had no intention of telling him. He felt desperate, and his fingers felt stiff and clumsy.

"I love your sister, Laura. I have to talk to her."

The set of her chin was stubborn and her eyes challenged him. "You break my sister's heart. Don't want it to happen second time."

He struggled for the right signs. "I know I hurt her really bad, and I'll try never to do it again. I want to marry her."

Laura's eyes dropped to her own bare ring finger. "Marrying is hard for Parker women."

Jackson had gone on at length during the last phone call, warning Kevin just how impossibly difficult the Parker women were about marriage.

"Well, I'm going to give it my best shot, anyway." He drew in a deep breath. "I have to be with her, whether she marries me or not. I'll follow her around and wear her down until she gives me a chance, Laura. I'll talk her into it."

"Stubborn. Like Jackson. But don't forget, she's really mad at you." She gave him a long, careful look. "Might shoot you instead of talking."

That possibility had crossed his mind.

"I'll take my chances." The baby was howling now at the top of his lungs. Kevin was going to have to bring it to Laura's attention soon. "Please, just tell me where she is, Laura?"

But she'd bent and looked in the window at the angry baby.

"Hungry again," she signed, and now she was getting into the car and starting it, just as he'd feared she would. He reached out and took her hand, forcing her to look at him. "Please, Laura?"

Her clear eyes suddenly shot dangerous sparks at him. "Hurt her again and I'll shoot you myself. She's at Grizzly Camp. Honeymoon Lake."

He made the graphic sign for "thank you" several times, but she was already driving away.

12

IT TOOK HIM A FULL DAY, but finally Kevin managed to rent a horse and assemble supplies, including a rifle. Jackson helped, and offered to haul Kevin and the horse as far as base camp.

"I know what you're goin' through, man," Jackson told him with a friendly thump on the shoulder. "Good luck, huh?"

Kevin figured he'd need it.

He remembered the seismic road to the river crossing well enough, and his horse, a well-mannered gelding called Charlie, forded the river without any problems. The Elk River was considerably lower than it had been in the spring, and Kevin was grateful. He told Charlie so at length. Being out in the wilderness alone like this was an unnerving experience.

Now, however, he had to try and remember where Emily had led them, once they'd crossed the Elk. Soon there was no discernible trail, and by late afternoon he knew he'd lost the way good and properly. He backtracked over and over and finally stumbled, quite by accident, on the blind turnoff in the middle of a rockslide where they'd headed off into the trees.

"We found it, Charlie, old son." Kevin felt jubilant. He'd had visions of wandering around up here for days or weeks.

But by now the sun was setting.

"Let's make camp, Charles, and we'll get an early start in the morning."

Funny, he'd never understood people who talked to their animals before, yet he'd been doing it himself all day. Obviously, this was a learning experience in more ways than one.

It wasn't much of a camp. The woods were tinder dry, so he didn't dare light a fire. Supper was cold sausage and dried-up sandwiches, with water as a chaser, and Kevin found that the pine boughs he'd cut for a bed were lumpy as hell. It was freezing bloody cold, and the coyotes began howling as soon as darkness fell. Once, a large animal crashed through the bush, seemingly only yards away, making Charlie nervous.

Kevin kept his rifle handy and didn't bother sleeping much at all. Instead, he thought about Emily, and the things that could happen to her, out in this godforsaken wilderness alone. If she agreed to marry him, he'd have to accept her life-style, he knew that. Could he live with a wife who thought nothing of heading off like this into the bush by herself? Hell, there were two-hundred-fifty-pound rugby players who wouldn't brave this country alone.

He wouldn't himself if it weren't for her. But he'd live in a tent out here if that's what she wanted. The summer without her had taught him all he wanted to know about loneliness.

Then he thought of the changes he'd made in his life because of Emily. He and Barney had a long way to go before they achieved anything like the relationship Gertrude had with her daughters, but at least the old man was opening up a little.

Hell, he'd even started talking about Kevin's mother, now and then—mostly when Kevin out-and-out forced him to. But they'd actually started taking the odd walk together in the evening or on a Sunday, and they only spent part of the time arguing about work.

Work. That was another thing. He'd taken a whole new attitude toward work lately, that was certain. He arrived later at the office and left sooner, and his life wasn't regimented by the clock anymore. He'd started taking photographs just for his own pleasure—shots of English Bay and faces of people he saw on the streets.

He'd developed all the pictures of Emily he'd taken, and enlarged them, every single one of them. They covered the walls of his small, barren apartment—color shots of her that were the last images he saw when he went to bed at night and the first things he looked for in the morning. Those pictures had helped him get through the summer—no doubt about it. And he'd kept busy; that had helped.

He'd wanted badly to come back right away, but he knew it was wiser to wait, to let some of her hurt and anger fade before he tried to win her over again. He'd spent the summer hoping she'd write, or even telephone; he knew it wasn't rational, but he went on hoping, anyway.

He'd been busy, all right, but the summer had also given him time to think, time to plot out a strategy that might appeal to her. He'd put more work and sweat into his plan for winning Emily over than he ever had in any business prospectus. He reviewed that plan now and waited, impatient and more than a little nervous, for dawn to break.

It was almost noon, and she'd just gotten up. She'd washed, and now she was making herself tea and toast. After falling asleep at dawn, she'd slept late, but it didn't really matter. There was nothing urgent for her to do, anyway.

The cabin door was open and the soft autumn morning spilled fresh air and warm sunshine inside. Birds were singing, and she heard Cody neigh out in the meadow.

Then she heard a horse approaching, and she scrambled for her rifle, conscious of being a woman and alone. She stepped outside.

He was already getting down from his horse, and he took a few steps toward her, eyeing the rifle warily.

"You're not really going to use that on me, are you, Em?"

He smiled at her, and she thought for an instant she was going to faint.

Her throat was dry, and her heart was hammering as though she was having an attack of some kind. Her whole body was trembling, and she'd entirely forgotten the rifle, still aimed more or less at his midsection.

"Kevin," she whispered, as hope and a delirious sort of joy wound through her. She cleared her throat and tried again. "What—what are you doing here? How did you get here?" she finally stammered.

He approached her slowly, and when he was close enough, reached out and took the rifle from her and laid it carefully on the ground behind him. He expelled his breath in a silent sigh of relief.

"How did you find me? Did Laura tell you? She must have, because she and Jackson are the only ones who knew where I'd gone."

He nodded, still not saying anything. He looked at her, from the top of her head down to her bare feet, as if he was memorizing every detail, and she realized that she hadn't bothered to brush her hair yet, or put her jeans on. She was still wearing the tracksuit she'd slept in, and she was naked underneath. Suddenly she felt vulnerable and a little shy.

Well, he'd seen her like this plenty of times before, she thought defiantly, lifting her chin and staring right back at him, trying not to grin.

God, he looked so good, even with a day's growth of beard on his chin and that rumpled look that suggested he'd slept in his clothes last night. There was a deep scratch on one cheek, and his eyes were bloodshot. There were lines around them that hadn't been there before, but there was also an expression in them of absolute determination.

"I found you a guiding territory, Emily," he burst out. "Up in the Caribou. It's a lot like this country, wild and untamed. I know you'll like it. Five thousand acres, plenty of game and fish, a couple of cabins, several lakes. The guy that had it is getting too old. He's got a good clientele he'll pass on to you."

Slowly it dawned on her, and she understood what he was saying.

It was incredibly simple. She'd been a fool not to guess right off. He just felt guilty. His conscience was bothering him, and he wanted to ease it. He needed to have her absolve him—that's what this was about. That's *all* it was about. *Here's another territory for you, Emily, and now I'm off the hook.*

For a moment her disappointment was almost more than she could bear. It was a good thing he'd taken the gun away, because at that moment she truly would have been capable of shooting him.

"You . . . you bastard. You . . ." She couldn't stand to look at him anymore. She didn't want to be anywhere near him. She started to run across the meadow toward the lake, ignoring the sharp, dry grass that prickled her bare feet. She wouldn't cry, she wouldn't.

She ran harder, gulping down the sobs that choked her.

"Emily. Em, what the hell . . . ?"

She heard him call, and she knew he was coming after her. She ran faster still, hating him.

He caught her just before she reached the lake, and she fought like a wildcat, using all her considerable strength and the force of her pent-up anger to strike out at him, kicking and punching and trying to knee him.

He was panting hard by the time he finally had her pinned beneath him. He straddled her, half sitting on her, his thighs and legs holding her body down, his hands tightly holding her wrists up over her head.

She was sobbing in earnest now—great gulping sobs that hurt her chest—and she shut her eyes so she wouldn't have to look into his face as she still writhed and twisted beneath him.

"Let—me—go."

"Emily, what in bloody hell is this all about?" He was yelling at her and breathing hard. "I come thousands of miles to see you—and you act like this. Jesus, Emily, I know what my company did hurt you. I know it was unforgivable of me to lie to you the way I did, but for God's sake, woman, I'm crazy in love with you. Can't you see that?"

He was absolutely furious. He was shaking her captured wrists and he was shouting. His voice echoed off the nearby peaks.

Still, she was certain she hadn't heard him right. She was making too much noise bawling, and his weight was crushing her. She stopped fighting and crying in order to listen, but she kept her eyes screwed shut. That way, she could concentrate better on what he was saying.

"I spent all goddamned summer flying around B.C., fighting my way through swamps and getting eaten alive by mosquitoes and blackflies, looking for somewhere—someplace—I could buy or lease that would make it up to you—someplace you might be able to learn to love the way you love this valley. It wasn't easy, believe me. I even got stalked by a cougar once, but I finally found a place, and now when I tell you about it, you go totally nuts on me." He drew in a deep breath and let it out slowly.

His tone was fierce and determined. "Well, I don't give a damn if it takes all winter and we starve, I'm going to keep you up here until you agree to marry me, woman. I'll…I'll…tie you up if I have to, do you hear me?" He sounded at the end of his rope. It was the first time she could ever remember him losing complete control of his temper.

She kind of liked it. He was altogether too reserved most of the time, anyway. Except when they were making love, of course.

"You damn Parker females, you're enough to drive men insane. You're all so stubborn. What the hell do you have against marriage, anyway?"

She opened her eyes and looked up at him. His hair was tousled, and his head was framed against the blue sky. His dark eyes were ferocious, and he was looking down at her and scowling.

"You're driving me out of my mind, Emily, do you know that?"

He didn't let her go, but his hold on her gentled, although his voice was still agitated and angry.

"I've got to travel a fair bit because of my job, but it doesn't matter where I live. Hell, there are fax machines and telephones and computers. If you hate the Caribou that much, then we'll find someplace else you do like. I have to supervise construction here in the Elk Valley for a long while, anyway, so we've got plenty of time."

The anger left his voice. "Or is this all because you don't love me, Em?"

There was raw vulnerability in his face. He released her hands abruptly and braced himself on the ground on either side of her, as if he was waiting for a blow.

"Don't be ridiculous," she sputtered, struggling to a sitting position and glaring at him as she pushed her hair back. "Of course I love you, you idiot. But when you said that about the Caribou, I thought you were just trying to buy me off. Why didn't you say then that you loved me? And anyway, I have to stay around here—I need to watch Alex grow up. And besides, one of the other outfitters, Martin Fowler, offered me a job guiding next fall. I might take it—the money's good. I can't leave this valley, Kevin. You ought to know that. I—"

He clamped a hand over her mouth, stopping the flow of words.

"But—will—you—marry—me?" He roared it out, and the echo was louder this time, seeming to come from all around them: Marry me...marry me...marry me....

She kept him waiting an endless moment. He seemed to have forgotten his hand was still over her mouth, but it didn't matter at all.

The sign for *yes* was easy—a folded fist moving vigorously up and down. She used both hands to express her enthusiasm.

It took him a while to realize he could kiss her while she signed it.

Once upon a time...

There was the best romance series in all the land—Temptation.

You loved the heroes of REBELS & ROGUES. Now discover the magic and fantasy of romance. Pygmalion, Cinderella and Beauty and the Beast have an enduring appeal—and are the inspiration for Temptation's exciting new yearlong miniseries, LOVERS & LEGENDS. Bestselling authors including Gina Wilkins, Glenda Sanders, JoAnn Ross and Tiffany White reweave these classic tales—with lots of sizzle! One book a month, LOVERS & LEGENDS continues in February 1993 with:

#429 WILDE AT HEART
Janice Kaiser
(Beauty and the Beast)

Live the fantasy....

LL2

HARLEQUIN®

Temptation

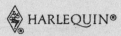

The most romantic day of the year is here! Escape into the exquisite world of love with MY VALENTINE 1993. What better way to celebrate Valentine's Day than with this very romantic, sensuous collection of four original short stories, written by some of Harlequin's most popular authors.

ANNE STUART
JUDITH ARNOLD
ANNE McALLISTER
LINDA RANDALL WISDOM

THIS VALENTINE'S DAY, DISCOVER ROMANCE WITH MY VALENTINE 1993

Available in February wherever Harlequin Books are sold. VAL93

OFFICIAL RULES • MILLION DOLLAR BIG BUCKS SWEEPSTAKES
NO PURCHASE OR OBLIGATION NECESSARY TO ENTER

To enter, follow the directions published. **ALTERNATE MEANS OF ENTRY:** Hand print your name and address on a 3" ×5" card and mail to either: Harlequin "Big Bucks," 3010 Walden Ave., P.O. Box 1867, Buffalo, NY 14269-1867, or Harlequin "Big Bucks," P.O. Box 609, Fort Erie, Ontario L2A 5X3, and we will assign your Sweepstakes numbers. (Limit: one entry per envelope.) For eligibility, entries must be received no later than March 31, 1994. No responsibility is assumed for lost, late or misdirected entries.

Upon receipt of entry, Sweepstakes numbers will be assigned. To determine winners, Sweepstakes numbers will be compared against a list of randomly preselected prizewinning numbers. In the event all prizes are not claimed via the return of prizewinning numbers, random drawings will be held from among all other entries received to award unclaimed prizes.

Prizewinners will be determined no later than May 30, 1994. Selection of winning numbers and random drawings are under the supervision of D.L. Blair, Inc., an independent judging organization, whose decisions are final. One prize to a family or organization. No substitution will be made for any prize, except as offered. Taxes and duties on all prizes are the sole responsibility of winners. Winners will be notified by mail. Chances of winning are determined by the number of entries distributed and received.

Sweepstakes open to persons 18 years of age or older, except employees and immediate family members of Torstar Corporation, D.L. Blair, Inc., their affiliates, subsidiaries and all other agencies, entities and persons connected with the use, marketing or conduct of this Sweepstakes. All applicable laws and regulations apply. Sweepstakes offer void wherever prohibited by law. Any litigation within the province of Quebec respecting the conduct and awarding of a prize in this Sweepstakes must be submitted to the Régies des Loteries et Courses du Quebec. In order to win a prize, residents of Canada will be required to correctly answer a time-limited arithmetical skill-testing question. Values of all prizes are in U.S. currency.

Winners of major prizes will be obligated to sign and return an affidavit of eligibility and release of liability within 30 days of notification. In the event of non-compliance within this time period, prize may be awarded to an alternate winner. Any prize or prize notification returned as undeliverable will result in the awarding of that prize to an alternate winner. By acceptance of their prize, winners consent to use of their names, photographs or other likenesses for purposes of advertising, trade and promotion on behalf of Torstar Corporation without further compensation, unless prohibited by law.

This Sweepstakes is presented by Torstar Corporation, its subsidiaries and affiliates in conjunction with book, merchandise and/or product offerings. Prizes are as follows: Grand Prize—$1,000,000 (payable at $33,333.33 a year for 30 years). First through Sixth Prizes may be presented in different creative executions, each with the following approximate values: First Prize—$35,000; Second Prize—$10,000; 2 Third Prizes—$5,000 each; 5 Fourth Prizes—$1,000 each; 10 Fifth Prizes—$250 each; 1,000 Sixth Prizes—$100 each. Prizewinners will have the opportunity of selecting any prize offered for that level. A travel-prize option, if offered and selected by winner, must be completed within 12 months of selection and is subject to hotel and flight accommodations availability. Torstar Corporation may present this Sweepstakes utilizing names other than Million Dollar Sweepstakes. For a current list of all prize options offered within prize levels and all names the Sweepstakes may utilize, send a self-addressed, stamped envelope (WA residents need not affix return postage) to: Million Dollar Sweepstakes Prize Options/Names, P.O. Box 4710, Blair, NE 68009.

The Extra Bonus Prize will be awarded in a random drawing to be conducted no later than May 30, 1994 from among all entries received. To qualify, entries must be received by March 31, 1994 and comply with published directions. No purchase necessary. For complete rules, send a self-addressed, stamped envelope (WA residents need not affix return postage) to: Extra Bonus Prize Rules, P.O. Box 4600, Blair, NE 68009.

For a list of prizewinners (available after July 31, 1994) send a separate, stamped, self-addressed envelope to: Million Dollar Sweepstakes Winners, P.O. Box 4728, Blair, NE 68009.

SWP-H393

ROMANCE IS A YEARLONG EVENT!

Celebrate the most romantic day of the year with MY VALENTINE! (February)

CRYSTAL CREEK
When you come for a visit Texas-style, you won't want to leave! (March)

Celebrate the joy, excitement and adjustment that comes with being JUST MARRIED! (April)

Go back in time and discover the West as it was meant to be . . . UNTAMED— Maverick Hearts! (July)

LINGERING SHADOWS
New York Times bestselling author Penny Jordan brings you her latest blockbuster. Don't miss it! (August)

BACK BY POPULAR DEMAND!!!
Calloway Corners, involving stories of four sisters coping with family, business and romance! (September)

FRIENDS, FAMILIES, LOVERS
Join us for these heartwarming love stories that evoke memories of family and friends. (October)

Capture the magic and romance of Christmas past with HARLEQUIN HISTORICAL CHRISTMAS STORIES! (November)

WATCH FOR FURTHER DETAILS IN ALL HARLEQUIN BOOKS!

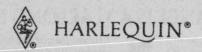# HARLEQUIN®

THE TAGGARTS OF TEXAS!

Harlequin's Ruth Jean Dale brings you
THE TAGGARTS OF TEXAS!

Those Taggart men—strong, sexy and hard to resist...

You've met Jesse James Taggart in FIREWORKS!
Harlequin Romance #3205 (July 1992)

And Trey Smith—he's THE RED-BLOODED YANKEE!
Harlequin Temptation #413 (October 1992)

Now meet Daniel Boone Taggart in SHOWDOWN!
Harlequin Romance #3242 (January 1993)

And finally the Taggarts who started it all—in LEGEND!
Harlequin Historical #168 (April 1993)

Read all the Taggart romances!
Meet all the Taggart men!

Available wherever Harlequin Books are sold.
